Life Is a Country Western Song

Life Is a Country Western Song

H. Lee Barnes

BAOBAB PRESS
RENO, NV

Typeset and Design © 2019 Baobab Press

First Printing

ISBN-13: 978-1-936097-20-3
ISBN-10: 1-936097-20-6

Library of Congress Control Number: 2018950306

Baobab Press
121 California Avenue
Reno, Nevada 89509
www.baobabpress.com

Printed in the United States

Because the true measure of success in life is the friends one makes, this book is dedicated to my longstanding colleagues and fellow writers Todd Moffett, Tina Eliopulos, Erica Vital, and Jacob Elison, who have generously offered me their meaningful and continued support.

contents

Life Is a Country Western Song

a fine open space

G rady began barking long before the pickup came into sight. Nevada stepped out of her double-wide and called to him from the porch, but by then the dog was racing off to the stalls where Pablo was repairing the gate. Somehow the latch had slipped free the day before and her gelding had loped off toward the highway. The animal had covered a half mile before Pablo managed to rope and return it to its stall. With all else that hung over her–a backlog of feed bills, a corroded well pump, and a hundred dollars due for the repair of a tattered saddle seat–she didn't need the worry of a broken fence and a runaway horse.

Nevada stood on the porch, watching the plume of dust billow up as the pickup bounded over the approach road. More and more going out, she thought, less and less coming in. Lately she'd questioned her choice, wondering at this very moment if repairing the saddle could have waited. When she took on the ranch she knew the life wouldn't be easy. She knew also because of her past life, she wouldn't fit in polite company. She needed this place, these open spaces to free herself of that past. Her hope then was that she'd make it here in the desolate flats some twenty miles east of the Kawich Range, one of the harder places in creation.

The former owner, a widower rancher with no children, had lived in a small trailer and died alone in it. His heirs–a niece, a dealer in Reno, and the nephew, a car salesman in Las Vegas–had no inclination to occupy the spread or pay taxes on the land. They sold all but fifty head of the cattle, paid the back taxes, and put the ranch up for sale. At two hundred dollars an acre, the fifty-four thousand price tag was in the range Nevada could afford. She'd sunk an additional forty-two thousand into birds and pens and a double-wide. She'd soon found that every dollar a ranch brought in was hard earned and easily lost. She'd needed all the rest of her nest egg to keep herself solvent until she could turn a profit off the place. She had no bull, so she farmed the breeding out to Sam Gorver who owned the Double-G, a three-thousand-acre spread to the north. Each year she'd managed to auction off enough steers to pay taxes, keep the ranch afloat, and employ Pablo, who at seventy-two was content to have Mr. Pender's trailer to sleep in and a two-hundred-dollar weekly wage. She'd been frugal wherever she could, scrimped on a swamp cooler for the home, ate oatmeal for breakfast and chicken breasts and pasta or beans for dinner.

Somehow Mr. Pender had scratched out a living despite the stubborn land. Nevada had experienced far less luck with raising cattle. She'd shifted her hopes to her growing flock of emu. She'd since found that she was competing with farmers in India who sold emu and exported their byproducts at cut rates. This year's weather had added to her problems. Winter had brought only scatterings of snow. When spring arrived, the blustering April winds blew cold and unrelenting from the northwest. In May they came from the southwest, warm and dry. The few cattle she still ranged had a tough go finding bunch grass, and she had to buy hay early and keep it spread at the watering tank.

Today, at least the air was still.

When the truck stopped a dozen feet from the trailer, Grady, tail wagging, came barking from the stalls and headed straight to the driver's door. The emu, numbering some four dozen, perked their heads. Some rose to their feet. Necks rocking, they strolled in circles and watched. She kept her old male, the surviving half of her seed pair, isolated from the hens who fought incessantly for his attention during mating season. And ever since the dog suffered a broken rib from a kick, a vet bill she paid in installments, she'd wired the bottom of the pen to keep him from the birds.

The diesel engine clattered and died. The driver's door opened and Stoney planted a booted foot tenderly on the ground before he stepped down on the hard pack. He bent down, gripped Grady's head in both hands, and playfully wrestled him back and forth. The dog broke free and immediately came back for more rough play. The ritual lasted a full half minute before Stoney patted the dog's head and walked toward Nevada, the dog trailing alongside him.

"Ever want to get rid of the worthless mutt, I'd consider taking him," he said.

"He's not worthless, just expensive."

Stoney stopped a few feet short of the trailer porch. "Morning."

"Same to you," she said.

"I got her done. Hope you like it." He pointed to the bed of the truck where a saddle rested atop a modified sawhorse. "Come see." Favoring his right leg, he ambled to the back of the truck and dropped the tailgate. She and the dog followed. Stoney mounted the running board, and climbed onto the bed, the effort and strain obvious.

"Bad hip," he said. "Time was I could climb up the back of a pickup when it was moving."

He freed the saddle from its ties and held it up for her inspection. It looked nearly new. As was the gelding, the saddle was part of the package when she purchased the two hundred and seventy acres of sand and caliche. Well-used when she'd inherited it, she'd since ridden the gelding until the saddle seat was frayed. Stoney had replaced the leather on the seat, but he'd also tooled a basket weave into the saddle skirt and fenders. Fix it, she'd told him, good leather, but keep it cheap. A new saddle or fancy tooling were indulgences she could ill afford.

"Didn't want carving," she said.

"You like it?"

"You said you'd turn the stirrup, put in a new tread and new leather on the seat. Nothing about fancy tooling. I'm not paying for it. One hundred to repair it. That's what we agreed on."

"Yes, ma'am. One hundred's right. I did the other just because. No charge. You like it?"

She turned away and looked at him from the corner of her eye. "I'm liking it better now."

"Well then, let me get it down so's you can get a good look. You been riding bareback?"

"Stoney, do I strike you as a woman who rides bareback." She was trim and though three years away from turning fifty, she looked more like a woman of forty.

"You look like you might be determined enough for it." He smiled and set the saddle on the side rail of the truck.

She looked at his hands as they balanced the saddle, knuckles

3

swollen, a few fingers disfigured. She wondered if they were painful. She reached for the saddle.

"I got it," he said. "I'll get myself down and take it into the tack room for you. "Where's that old Mexican? I brought him something."

"What?"

"Oh, some magazines. Come across them in Beatty. Mexican magazines."

"That's nice of you. I'll fix some iced tea if you got time."

"Nothing hanging over me." He walked to the tailgate and eased himself to the ground.

"Grady, come," she said.

The dog wagged his tail and stationed himself beside the truck. Having company was a rare adventure for the collie-lab mix. Nevada shrugged and went inside. She took two glasses from the cupboard and opened the freezer compartment. Grady began barking. How, she wondered, can a dog turn a walk to the tack room into a carnival? She smiled. It wasn't much, this life she'd taken on, but at times she found small pleasure in it, like the freedom of waking up in the morning and brushing her hair, then tying it in a ponytail. She'd barely touched makeup or lipstick for seven years now, and then only to do business. No mask, no pretensions. She scooped ice cubes into the glasses and set them on the table, then looked out the window. She saw Stoney reach inside the truck cab and hand some magazines to Pablo, who seemed pleased to receive them. Stoney pointed to the trailer. Pablo nodded and headed in the direction of the stalls, Grady, tail at full wag, leading the way.

She opened the door. Stoney stood in the threshold, in his hand a magazine. He extended it to her.

"What's this?"

"Latest *American Horseman*. Thought you might like something to read. You don't seem the kind who reads *Better Homes and Gardens*."

"Guess that's one way of judging a person. Well, that's nice of you. Come in."

They sat at the table sipping cold tea. She knew him mostly through services he'd rendered her in the past. Mr. Pender's niece had given her Stoney's phone number and recommended him as a jack of all trades, "All ranch trades, that is." He was farrier, saddlemaker, and horse trainer, and had once been a cowboy. The real deal. The niece added that Stoney was the one who'd found her uncle dead.

Stoney swirled the ice in his empty glass. Nevada asked if he wanted more.

He shook his head. "How's business with those ostriches going?"

"They're emu. Smaller and more feathered."

"Yes, ma'am. I suppose I should be going. How's that Dodge doing?"

"It's running rough again."

"Want me to take a look?"

"Pablo doesn't seem to have a handle on it."

"I'll take that as a maybe."

"No, go ahead. I need to keep it running. Friday, I have to deliver two females to a buyer. I got to meet him in Hawthorne."

"Emu?"

"What else?"

"Well, cattle. And you got cats all over the place."

"And no mice. Why'd you fancy up the saddle?"

"Ah, I had that tooled leather hanging around the shop. Working on leather takes my mind off my hip. Beats dulling it with Jack D like I did for too long a time. I'll go look at that truck."

She handed him the keys to the Dodge and walked him to the door. She had a day's chores that needed tending and a gelding that needed riding. She left the dirty glasses in the sink. An hour later Stoney approached her as she was watering some tomato plants.

"I think your fuel line's fouled. And you've got a crack in your exhaust manifold."

"Can you fix it now?"

"The fuel line, but—"

"I need that truck running."

"If it can't be welded good, I'll do what I can to get you a manifold cheap."

Again, she thought, everyone, the banker, the vet, thinks I've got money to throw away. She had to sell two female birds just to pay the coming month's utility bills, groceries, gas for the truck. She'd forgotten the times her new life pleased her.

"Okay. Let me know how much."

"Well, I can fix the fuel line in exchange for another glass of tea."

🌵 🌵 🌵 🌵 🌵 🌵

THAT FRIDAY AT EIGHT a.m. Stoney called with news that the manifold hadn't arrived. His news capped off what had been a sleepless night. As she did too often, she'd stewed on the past, this time the confounding interludes she endured as Raja employed his tools of seduction, humiliation, and threats combined with loving caresses and praise.

After hanging up the receiver, Nevada sat at the table, her head in her hands, wondering how she was going to handle the delay. She decided to call Phil Redmond and tell him she'd have to postpone the deal for a week or so and see if she could convince him to make the drive down to the ranch. He lived in Lemmon Valley north of Reno and said that since they'd managed to meet the price halfway, they could do the same with the exchange, halfway being Hawthorne.

Before she could dial, the phone rang and Stoney's voice was on the other end of the line.

"The manifold come in?" she asked.

"No."

"Then why the hell you call me again? To tell me you still don't have a manifold?"

"Huh? I, I just, I—"

She heard him breathing heavily as if calming himself. She started to apologize, but he spoke up first. "I called to say I got nothing pressing on me. I'll be pleased to drive you and them birds to Hawthorne. I mean, if that's okay."

"Okay? Hell, Stoney, that's good of you. When can you come?"

"I'm leaving now. How's that?"

"Perfect. I'm sorry I snapped at you."

She added her goodbye to his, laid the receiver down, and stared at the ceiling for a moment, letting the sense of relief flow through her. At moments like these, moments that didn't happen often because she kept herself busy, she remembered what she'd escaped. Seven years into her new life and still the old one overtook her. She'd wonder about the girls, the pimps, but never the tricks. They swirled into the same murky ebbtide. She rubbed her eyes and stood. Grady wagged his tail.

"Let's go get the birds ready," she said. *Let's do anything*, she thought.

She and Pablo caged the emu, rigged the pulleys on the hoist, and threaded rope through the top of each cage. Pablo asked several times if she was all right. The way his suspendered trousers sagged over his butt, his slow response to questions, everything about his appearance said he was old, except for his dark, intense eyes. He often seemed concerned about her, but it served her to think that was because she was his meal ticket. It was best to keep their relationship at a distance. She said that she was fine and told him to stop asking. When all was set for Stoney's arrival, she returned to the trailer and sat on the porch drinking coffee and stroking Grady's neck.

Stoney drove in a little past nine. He stepped out of the pickup and stood in the sunlight. He wore a hat she'd never seen on him, a fine wool Stetson and a neatly pressed shirt and jeans so new they shined. He waved, then sauntered over to the porch.

She looked at his boots, Luccheses, freshly polished, "What's the occasion?" she asked.

"Occasion?"

"Yeah, you're dressed to go dancing."

"Haven't done that for a while," he said.

He seemed embarrassed. She suddenly felt self-conscious of her own appearance. In the intervening years since leaving Lyon County, she'd worn a dress just a handful of times and then only to sign deeds and legal documents. Years ago, her appearance had been her currency, but that was when what a man wanted mattered.

"Coffee?" she asked.

"That'd be appreciated."

They finished off the pot, after which he went outside and backed his pickup to the hoist. Pablo and Stoney loaded the cages on the bed. Nevada went to her closet and took a spring dress with spaghetti straps off a hanger. In front of the mirror she held the dress tight to her breasts. Since she'd last worn it, she'd lost ten pounds or more. It would fit loosely. That too once would have mattered, but now she didn't care. She stepped out of her jeans, unbuttoned her dungaree work shirt, and slipped the dress over her head. Standing sideways, she looked at her image, took in her bruised calves, the scratches on her arms, the suntan line on her throat left by the open collar of her work shirts, and she saw her terribly pale shoulders.

She flung the dress on her bed, bent over, and stepped into the legs of her jeans. Before stepping out, she made two concessions to appearance. She left her work shirt piled on the floor of the closet, selected a blue blouse that she tucked into the jeans, then she untied her ponytail and let her hair cascade over her shoulders. As a last touch, she crowned her head with a white Stetson she'd worn only once before.

Stoney waited at the steps. He looked at her and nodded. "Ready?"

"No," she said, "I just came out to see if the day was still here."

He smiled, opened her door, and stepped aside.

He said little until they passed through Tonopah, then as if some long-wound spring had been triggered inside him, he started talking, first about his boyhood. He'd been reared in east-central Nevada and had been on horses ever since he could remember.

"My mother said I rode alone the first time when I was two. I don't know if there's truth in it, but that's what she said. Sometimes I wonder if it'd all been different if I'd finished school. Wasn't a bad student, just had other ambition, which really wasn't ambition at all. How about you?"

"How about me, what?"

"Were you raised on a ranch or—"

"You were doing just fine talking about yourself."

He glanced at her, blinked once, then faced the road, his jaw tense. It wasn't until they were ten miles north of Tonopah that he spoke again. "I apologize. You're entitled to privacy. It's just people on the road usually talk more freely. You know, to pass time."

She nodded.

"I don't mean no harm," he said. "Just curious. Just passing time. Hell, I picked up hitchhikers who told me their life story in an hour, some of which might even have been true. There's them that lie and them that just hold back the truth. Take your pick."

She thought of men who'd spilled deep feelings to her, strangers who'd wanted someone to talk to about their lives as much as they'd wanted sex. Some lived in homes that were lies. Some lived lonely lives in the midst of family.

"Not everyone's a liar," she said, "Some people just talk to strangers."

"True. Thought you might want to talk yourself, but maybe you don't have a story."

"Why would you say that? Just because I don't babble on and on?"

"Some babble in their heads." He grinned and looked in the rear-view mirror. "Pender, he was a good man. We called him Buck. Did you know that?"

She gazed at the roadside where a westerly wind pressed against the sage and creosote. *Talk*, she thought, *and drive. Just get me there by eleven.* He was, after all, doing her a kindness. If he seemed compelled to talk, fine. Besides, it took her mind off . . . well, a lot.

"I think I heard his niece call him that," she said, trying to encourage him along.

"Not much caring there. I saw the niece maybe twice in a dozen years. Met the nephew at the funeral. Families. Hell, I was more family than them. He treated me like a son sometimes, but told me if he'd sired me–his words–he would've felt obligated to cut his privates off for fear of duplicating the mistake. Always had more work for me than he had money to pay. Kept his copper real close to his yarn, he did. I liked him enough. Didn't matter his habits with a dollar. He was a good cook too. He'd have us beans and steaks cooked on an open fire when we'd brand and castrate the calves. Miss that old man sometimes. Do you cook?"

She'd never cooked before buying the ranch. Restaurants, coffee shops, order-out food, and later, in the houses, food and house-cleaning were provided. "I'm learning."

"Always thought Old Buck was stingy, but look." He turned to her and stretched his mouth open wide, exposing his teeth and gums for an instant before returning his eyes to the road. "Buck did it for me. A toothbrush ain't the first thing a man reaches for when he's rid-ing fence or bent over coals heating a branding iron. Eight implants, didn't even know what they were until he put it in his will for me to get them. Twenty-two thousand it cost. Damn near wiped out all the money he left behind. Course the niece and nephew got the land, the cattle, and some cash. You got some scrawny four-legged leftovers."

She chuckled, then thought about what he'd said, the mention of family. She pictured the bus terminal next to the Union Plaza, six dollars in her clutch purse, her sitting on a plastic chair, on her lap an overnight bag with two pairs of jeans, two tank tops, her dirty underwear, and a bus ticket to Orange County in her hand. Raja stepped into the terminal, scanned the room, and zeroed in on her immediately. Pimp radar. He sat next to her pretending at first not to notice her, then asking her where she was headed. Ever since, she'd wondered countless times what her life might have been if she'd not answered *nowhere*–in the end a prophetic word.

Stoney glanced at her. "Did I offend you? I mean, saying what he said?"

"No. Tell me more. Go ahead."

"He made good money drilling water wells as a side business. Never ran more than three hundred head. That's how I come to work for him."

She drifted between his story and hers, Stoney sitting in the tack room, sharing a bottle of Jack Daniel's with Buck, herself lying in bed with Sonya who pulled her close and assured her she would be cared for, that they were like sisters now.

"Can I ask you something?"

Her hands tensed. "Sure."

"You have family anywhere?"

She recalled the argument over her wrecking the family car that sent her drifting, first San Francisco, Los Angeles, then Las Vegas, sometimes panhandling, sometimes bussing tables.

"Everyone has family," she said.

"Buck said that if we don't have one, we find one. You think that's true?"

"Maybe." She imagined Raja riding in the truck bed, framed in the rear window, reading her mind. He had told her his exotic name, and his dark hand was warm as he laid it atop hers. She'd felt helpless to resist. He'd fed her in the dining room of the Union Plaza, and said he knew her every thought and her fears. She weighed ninety pounds then. Ninety pounds and seventeen. A child. Now a bitter image.

"You alright?" he asked. "You drifted off there."

"I'm fine. Do you have family?"

"Parents dead. Got a brother and sister. He's gone crazy. She's gone Mormon. Same thing, some people might say."

She smiled and thought that Stoney would make good company. For someone, not her.

"We're almost there."

"Good. Did I thank you for this?"

"What?"

"Thank you for taking me and the birds. Did I thank you?"

"I'm sure you did."

She studied his profile, the sunbaked lines at the corner of his eyes and mouth, his forehead shadowed by the brim of his Stetson. "Really. I'm not so sure I did."

"Well, then. You know, it's never too late."

"Okay. Thank you. I'll buy you a meal at the El Capitan."

"Call it even."

"What happened to your hands."

"Just about everything that can happen to hands, short of losing fingers." He changed grips on the steering wheel and extended his right hand toward her. "Old Buck's will was a million short of having enough money to fix them up." He extended the baby finger. "Roped a bull. Big bastard went in one direction, horse went in another. Something had to give. This finger snapped and bent back almost to my wrist."

"That must have been a trip to the emergency room."

"Naw, I pulled it straight as I could and had Bud Hickum fix me up a splint. I was working the next day, but not roping nothing from a horse for a time." He let his free hand rest palm up on the seat.

Nevada had seen hands as weathered and beaten as his, carpenters missing fingers, mechanics with broken nails, cooks bearing burn scars, all of their hands blurring into one. And the others, the ones with soft hands, bankers, accountants, executives. She couldn't imagine the hard life a man like Stoney endured. Any scars from her labor were less conspicuous. Until now. She'd learned to use a hammer and a saw. A shovel or rake was in her hands most days. She wore gloves, except in the peak of the summer when it was too hot sometimes to breathe.

She listened to the tires whistle on the hardtop as the highway faded in the sideview mirror. She considered that she'd be seeing the same land again on the return trip. Stretch after stretch of tar cutting across empty desert. She knew the drive well enough, but sitting as she was on the passenger side it seemed different. She found it disquieting to consider how she viewed herself. As in a mirror's view moving away? Or as someone heading toward something?

For the next several minutes the whistling tires and the sound of wind skirting the truck cab lulled her into a near daze, then he broke the silence. "If you want, I can get us some music."

"No. I'm fine."

"Do you have a sister? Maybe a brother?"

"No. Neither."

She lowered her eyes and pictured the Bible clasped between Raja's hands, him instructing her and Sonya to lay their hands on his. Sonya and she would be sisters. It was now sanctified by him and God. And he would be one in spirit with them. Raja had taken her to a motel on East Fremont Street, but didn't touch her that first night. In the morning, he gave her a pill he claimed would give color to the day and he introduced her to Sonya, saying God had willed her to him and Sonya, that they were now a family. He'd searched her purse, found the unused bus ticket and he tore it up, letting the pieces scatter on the floor. Then he traced the word love on the back of her hand with a fingernail, said that her name was no longer Diane but Mara, like the moon. Then he'd slapped her and told her to pick up the pieces of her ticket and throw them away.

As a girl, she'd lain "together in the pasture of delight" with Raja and Sonya, she'd cried and bled on the sheets, and he'd told her to take them to a laundry to wash them clean before she could eat or sleep again. The following night, she and Sonya returned from Caesars Palace with the night's take and Raja had slapped her because she'd cried and because someone pure as she should "bring home a little more bacon."

"Lost you again."

She lifted her eyes and looked at Stoney. "I'm here. If you want to turn on the radio, go ahead."

"You never answered the question. You know, about the past?"

"It's something I don't discuss."

"Suit yourself. Way I see it, we get a certain age, the past is mostly what we got to talk about."

"Then we should all be young forever." She reached in her purse and pulled out a packet of chewing gum. She offered him a stick. He shook his head and said gum stuck to his implants.

"Hell." He tapped the brake, slowed the truck, and aimed one of his mangled fingers at the highway ahead. "Accident."

She looked at the string of taillights. Cars and trucks jammed together loomed ahead on either side of the highway. Nevada looked at her watch and shook her head. Hawthorne was forty miles down the road and eleven o'clock was forty-two minutes away. The simple life she'd fostered seemed to get more complicated despite her best efforts.

"I hope it's not going to make us late." She looked back at the emu.

Two Highway Patrol cars, a tow truck, and a crushed car crowded into the northbound lane, and no one was directing traffic around the accident. Stoney pulled the truck to a stop at the rear of some fifteen vehicles.

"Even more cars trying to get south," he said. "You wait here." He reached under his seat and came up with a two-foot-long flashlight. "I'll be back." He shut the door gently, walked to the shoulder, and headed toward the accident, the heels of his boots sinking into the sand. She noticed that he was slightly bowlegged.

For a time, she lost sight of him. Soon, one at a time, cars heading south began to pass by the truck. Then gradually the vehicles in front of the truck advanced. She saw Stoney standing on the crown of the highway directing them forward. It made her smile.

Fifteen minutes later he opened the door and climbed up behind the wheel. "Ambulance come and left already. No one was killed."

"You just walked up there and volunteered?"

"Yeah, might be a bit longer yet. They towed the truck that hit it already. Said I'd help out until that car's gone to the graveyard. Maybe an hour. That okay?"

Where does someone like him come from? she wondered. She wanted to tell him to forget helping, that he'd done his share and earned the right to go on, but she figured that he wouldn't agree she was right even if he went along with her, and she'd have to make the long trip back with that hanging between them.

"I guess."

"I told them you wouldn't mind."

He drove just north of the accident site and parked the truck. "This way we can just take off."

"Where'd you get the ostriches?" one of the troopers hollered as Stoney walked to the center of the pavement.

"Emu, not ostriches. They're shorter and got more feathers. Don't they teach you cops nothing at all?"

A semi rolled up to the scene, and Stoney motioned for it to wait as one of the troopers stepped out onto the asphalt with a measuring device.

THEY ARRIVED TEN MINUTES after the scheduled rendezvous time. As prearranged, Phil Redmond was waiting in the east parking lot of the El Capitan with a ranch hand named Lou and two empty cages. Stoney backed his truck close enough to Redmond's to drop the tailgate and the three men lifted the empty cages to the back of the truck. Lou, a young Shoshone with a broad forehead and muscular shoulders, harnessed the birds one at a time and pulled them into the waiting cages. Stoney and Lou chatted as they muscled the heavy cages to the front of the truck bed, Phil handed Nevada an envelope containing two thousand in hundred-dollar bills. Without opening it, she tucked the envelope in her purse.

"You didn't count it?"

"No." Nevada knew a man was likely to cheat a woman when selling something, but only the worst kind of man cheated a woman when buying, like the few johns who'd used her, then stiffed her.

"Expensive day," he said. "This Stoney, nice guy. He a boyfriend or an employee?"

"Neither. Just a guy with a pickup."

"Mr. Redmond, we're ready," Lou called out.

"Well, he's a nice guy all the same." Mr. Redmond opened his wallet and thumbed out a hundred-dollar bill. "Here, give it to him." He stuffed the money in the side pocket of her purse.

"I'm curious. Do you intend to breed them? I've got a couple of males for sale or for stud."

"No, I just wanted them for my kids to ride."

It wasn't what she'd expected to hear. "Really?"

"It'll be an adventure for them. I figure they'll love it. Have a nice day." He touched the brim of his hat and nodded as he backpedaled.

"Mr. Redmond?"

"Phil, call me Phil."

"I thought you were a rancher."

"I've got two hats, three, no, four, if you count being a husband

and father. I'm mostly an attorney: wills, probate, taxes. You ever need a good one, call."

"Sure."

A lunch crowd filled booths and most of the tables in the El Capitan. Stoney removed his hat. Nevada kept hers on. Though she'd bought the ranch as much to hide from people as to build a business, Nevada sometimes missed crowds and noise. They waited at the podium to be seated. She was hungry now and Stoney seemed finally to have run out of words. Nevada took in the sounds of slot-machine handles and the piped-in music, sounds that quickly took her back to that first walk through the slot aisles at Caesars Palace, her a girl full-breasted and tall who could pass for being a woman. Sonya had pointed to a man, faceless now, neither old nor young, a stranger away from home with money enough. Any man would've done—any who wasn't a cop, that is. She remembers his smell more than anything, sweat and an aftershave balm that seemed too sweet for a man to wear. It was odd how she most remembered the first and the last.

The hostess seated them at a table near the counter.

Stoney, his face locked in contemplation, looked around the room as if debating what to say. She noticed age spots on his sun-darkened forehead. He shook his head and studied the menu for a few seconds.

"A three-egg Denver omelet and wheat toast'll suit me. And coffee."

"Sounds fine."

"Maybe it's not my business," he said.

Nevada waited, but Stoney left the comment hanging. The waitress came, poured them coffee, and took their order. Nevada noticed a man at the counter looking over his shoulder in their direction. He looked away when she made eye contact. Stoney sipped from his cup and said the coffee was just brown water.

"What's not your business?"

"It's peculiar to me is all. That boy with Mr. Redmond said Redmond bought his kids some kind of buggy to have the birds pull them around. Maybe race. That seem strange?"

"No stranger than selling emu oil as a cure for arthritis or the FDA telling me I can't render my own birds to meat and sell it."

"What I mean is kids having them big birds as toys. Why not horses?"

She started to say she didn't have an answer, that maybe there was no answer, but the man at the counter was staring now. She found it disconcerting. He was her age, perhaps a few years older, well over two hundred pounds, his forearms sunburned. He wore construction boots and Levi's, could've been a working man anywhere in the outreaches of the state.

"What's wrong? Did I say something again?" Stoney said.

"No. I'm just hungry."

"Kids like that probably already have horses. Maybe they got bored with them. Kids get bored real easy now."

She remembered the hundred-dollar bill Phil Redmond had stuffed in her purse. She reached for her purse on the chair beside her and she saw the man slide off his stool. He stood looking at her as he opened his wallet and dropped a bill on the counter top. She didn't know him, but she recognized the type. He grinned at her and approached the table, looming behind Stoney's chair as he gazed down at Nevada. Bile rose up from her stomach. Blood rushed to her face and then withdrew like a riptide.

Stoney looked up and behind at the man. "Can we help you?"

"Just wanted to say hello to Chartreuse here. Remember me?"

Chartreuse was the last in a string of working names. The pulse at her temple hammered. She choked out the words. "No, I don't know you."

"Her name is Nevada. You got the wrong gal."

"No. Got the right one," he said, his voice rising. "She got me thrown out of a house."

She had a memory of walking the trick along the pathway to the back trailers. He'd grabbed her hand and something in her went haywire. She'd ripped her hand away from his grip. In the trailer, he'd pulled her to him and demanded she kiss him and for her to say the words "I love you." She'd shaken her head. No love to give, no words to express it, not to a trick, not to one more pimp, not to anyone. What he'd paid for was sex.

"Sex!" she'd shouted. "That's it."

"Say it!"

She'd said she loved him, but when his arms relaxed, she'd pressed a button to alert the madam. The bouncer and the madam had found her seated cross-legged on the linoleum, tears streaking her makeup.

"Mister, we're just trying to have a meal," Stoney said.

"What's the matter, Chartreuse? You can't talk?"

Others in the coffee shop were staring now. The hostess stepped over to the table and asked if there was a problem.

The man smiled. "No. Just stopped by to say hello to this whore here."

"She ain't a whore," Stoney said. He turned to stand.

"Stoney, don't," Nevada said. "Whoever you are, just go away."

The man, still smiling, backpedaled and headed to the street exit. Save for the music, the restaurant had gone silent. Some people nearby glanced at them discreetly. Others pretended the incident away.

"Let's leave," Nevada said.

"I got to go to the bathroom first," Stoney said.

"Okay. Then let's leave."

Gradually the sound of muffled voices and the utensils on plates along with the piped-in music and the slot buzzers filled the room again. She waited, the past like a vise squeezing her sides, no ends to her history, except for loose ones. The other patrons soon lost interest in her. They might retell the incident sometime in the future, recounting it with some speculation, a story lacking the nuance and truth only she knew.

Three minutes passed by, then four and five. Nevada saw a woman approach the hostess and point in her direction. There was quick exchange between them, then the hostess hurried over at the same time the waitress came with their orders.

"More coffee?" the waitress asked.

"We're leaving," Nevada said.

"Your friend," the hostess said. "That woman says he's outside on the sidewalk, hurt."

Nevada fumbled in her purse and pulled out the hundred-dollar bill intended for Stoney. She handed it to the hostess and hurried off without waiting for the change.

A man and a woman stood over Stoney, who lay on his back, blood trickling from the side of his head where he'd struck the concrete. A strawberry-colored lump had sprouted on his left eye.

"He came to for a bit then—" the man said.

"You stupid, stupid man." Nevada sat on the curb and lifted his head.

"That guy was a lot bigger than him," the man said.

"It's ugly the way he just left him," the woman said.

Stoney blinked. He looked at Nevada, then the others. He sat up and felt the side of his head. His fingers came away with blood. "I'll be damned," he said.

"Why'd you do … ? I should leave you lying here."

"We called the police," the woman said.

"My hat," Stoney said. "I left it inside."

THE DOCTOR'S OFFICE WAS a converted wooden bungalow near the military base. The doctor applied four stitches to the wound and cautioned her not to let Stoney sleep for at least a day, saying there were indications he'd suffered a concussion. The bill came to nearly four hundred dollars. She paid it out of the proceeds from the sale of her birds. After Stoney was bandaged and ready to leave, the police interviewed him. He declined to sign a complaint, saying he couldn't recall what had happened and couldn't identify the man the police referred to as the assailant.

Stoney walked to the truck on his own, apologizing as he did and thanking her for paying the doctor. "You don't worry about that manifold or paying me to install it. We'll call it even."

"Even? Don't you see what you did?"

"Got myself hurt." He opened the passenger door and motioned for her to get in.

"What the hell?" she said. "You get in. I'm driving."

"My hat."

They ate dinner at the El Capitan. The manager handed over Stoney's hat and the change from the bill for the uneaten meal. On the drive back, she had to nudge Stoney awake from time to time. For long moments, he was alert. At other times, his eyes got bleary as he drifted away. She urged him to talk, flipped station to station on the radio and turned up the volume until the speakers vibrated. She honked the horn. Once, she stopped the truck and walked him into the desert and back again. He touched the top of his bare head and asked where his hat was.

"It won't fit over the bandage," she said.

It was a little past eight when she pulled the truck onto the access road. The light in Pablo's window was a welcome sign. She'd need help taking care of Stoney. Grady sat on the porch, ears perked. She pulled to a stop and honked. Pablo came out, straightening his suspenders as he hurried to the truck.

"Let's get him inside," she said.

Stoney was as compliant as a sleepy child. She fixed a pot of coffee. When it was ready, she poured him a cup and coaxed him to sip until it was gone. She and Pablo took turns walking him outside around the pens and back. On one walk around the pens, one of the females stretched her head over the fence and released a chilling rattle. In the adjacent pen, a male sat on the egg she'd laid. Nevada told Stoney that the males mind the eggs and the females fight for the attention of males. He didn't seem to hear at the time, but later said that maybe people should learn from it.

Between alternately walking Stoney, she and Pablo napped in one-hour spans. At four in the morning, Stoney seemed to make a turn. "You can take me home," he said. "That manifold's probably in by now. I'll fix your truck up and bring it back. You can use mine until then."

"Was it worth it, Stoney?"

He thought a moment, then said, "Guess it's in what you value."

"Chartreuse was just one name," she said. "There were others."

"Only name I know is Nevada."

"I paid an attorney to give me that name. You still think it was worth it? Worth going after him to defend a whore, one a fool knew by the name of Chartreuse?"

He gazed at her as if digesting her words, then smiled. "Hell, I don't know anyone you'd call that. I know a good woman scratching a hard dollar out of hard land, and that's someone to respect. Besides, I didn't lose any teeth, did I? New teeth. New name. Don't seem so different. Both were changes for the good."

She felt something grow inside her, something she hadn't felt for years, something she could barely remember feeling, a reaction of sorts like the way some movies ended not in despair but moving toward a hopeful resolution. She took in a deep breath.

"I should take you home."

"Sure. You ever think of a ball? I mean a big one?"

"Maybe you need more coffee and another walk." She was suddenly aware that she'd been smiling nonstop since he'd improved. She wasn't angry. That surprised her. Four hundred dollars gone, she should be. "No, I can't recall thinking about a ball, why?"

"Well, when one's on the ground and you go to pick it up, where do you pick it up by?"

"The bottom?"

"Uh-huh. And what happens to that bottom once you've picked it up?"

Now she was grinning and helpless to stop herself from it. "Your head's more than injured. I don't know. What happens to it."

"Well, it's still there, but it sort of disappears because it's only the bottom temporarily."

"Huh?"

"Think about it. I mean, after you take me home. I'm fine now. And yes, it was worth it."

"If you say so."

"I do. Say, do you ever dance? I mean, go to dances?"

Yes, she'd danced, danced for men, sometimes naked, or for fun danced with other women in the houses, but she'd only been to two actual dances, those in high-school, prom dances. The car accident was after the second one, the accident that finally made her flee her home.

"No. I've danced, but—"

"Well, they's a dance twice a month. Saturdays. You might . . . I mean, I'd like to take you sometime. We don't have a lot more for entertainment here. But then . . . well, maybe I could take you sometime to this place down by Death Valley where a lady puts on a one-person play. Shakespeare mostly, but she played Molly Brown too. At least she did once."

She glanced at him. He was smiling now, smiling too broadly for her to say anything that would break the mood. "Who's Molly Brown?"

"The Unsinkable Molly Brown. Didn't go down with the *Titanic*. Like you, she carved herself a place in the West. Colorado. Fulfilled a dream."

Like me, she thought. Her place was never a dream and certainly wasn't now. It was an ambition, an escape, a fresh identity, never a dream. She hadn't had a dream like that since the one that drove her to run away. That dream had been to find a family that would love her and protect her. What she'd found was something quite different. Now she dreamed only in her sleep and those were often dreams of that dark past.

It was still dark when she dropped him off. His house was a small wood bungalow, the kind slapped together to accommodate miners and their families in Beatty's heyday. Unlike most of its kind, his was in good repair. He invited her in to see it. But she declined.

"Some day?" he asked. "And think about that dancing. I know I don't look much like I'd be a dancer, lame as I am, but I can get around. Live music too. The real country western, not that new stuff that's all about pickups and–"

He was staring at her, his face calm, his eyes expectant. He reached out with his hand and touched her shoulder. She fought back the urge to flinch and let his hand rest there.

"You're a good woman, taking care of me the way you did. I caused you more problems than I gave you help."

"We're fine, Stoney."

He pulled his hand away. "Well, think about my offer."

She watched him limp his way up to the porch, then drove to her ranch, her thoughts wavering between the previous day's events, her past, and the odd image of a ball and the idea of dancing. Every thought circled back to the day she should have used that bus ticket to take her home and at the same time fearing to return.

A ball? More words to trick people? Make them doubt their own minds. As she had hundreds of times over the years, she sifted through the events that had shaped her, but now she was seeking something tangible to carry forward from her long-ago experiences. What was the lesson? That people use people? That a human is just meat? That a person can change? Didn't Raja sell her to Alonso to settle a debt? Passed from one violent man to another and then another. A dozen pimps. A dozen names. In her late twenties she'd wondered if her parents were still worried about her. She called home to tell them she was alive. "Not to us," her father had said. At thirty-one, she learned the one lesson that mattered from an accountant who couldn't perform in bed. He'd convinced her that if she saved enough money, she could save herself or at least be free of men who paid for sex and the others who used her.

Exhausted but too wired from events to sleep, she sat on the edge of her bed and pictured Stoney limping along on his bowed legs, a wiry, middle-aged man, determined to clear traffic and get her to her destination. After a time, she left the bed and heated coffee, then sat in the darkened kitchen sipping at the cup. Could she dream while awake again? When the sun rose over the peaks, she slipped on her sunglasses and stepped outside where she met a cool breeze from the east. For years she'd made the idea of wide open spaces her sole dream, and now as she looked out over the vast tableland cast amber in morning sunshine, she tightened her hands into fists and smiled. Work lay ahead, as did other matters that demanded her attention. She'd forgotten to tell Stoney what a fine job he'd done with her saddle. That was something she figured he might want to hear. More important, it was something she should tell him, maybe over a slow meal or a slow ride on horseback over an open stretch of land or while on their way to hear a country western band play the old songs.

disassembled parts

Before Les decided to pursue matters, he'd read the profile beneath the photo several times, every sentence written in grammatical and clear prose, nothing overstated, little revealing who the attractive woman of fifty-two really was. Her name was Mona, a name that reminded him of the alluring actresses in the 1940s noir films he'd loved watching on television as a boy. Their first emails had been tentative–I-liked-your-photo and you-seem-interesting comments. Those were soon replaced by longer, more revealing messages sent every other day. She read fiction and memoirs and enjoyed foreign films, wine, and summer trips to Utah to see the Shakespeare Festival. Finally, they'd exchanged phone numbers and left messages on each other's answering machines. The pattern continued for three weeks without the two of them connecting. When she finally answered, he said, "I thought I was going to have to perform a seance to get in touch with you." She'd laughed and said that was funny, the exact right response.

Two months had passed since that first email. Once again, he turned on the computer and studied the expression on her face in the photo she'd posted and thought she appeared younger than her years. No matter, the one he'd posted was four years old, the last taken of him before Darlene died. It was time. She was the proper age, seemed to be a woman that Darlene would've approved of. They had so many things in common that it seemed delaying matters would be a mistake. On a Friday, Les proposed dinner the next night. She said that was fine, that she was free. He'd not dated for twenty-three years, so that afternoon he consulted his niece, who suggested an Indian restaurant. She said the food and service were excellent. It was on Paradise Road across from the Hard Rock Casino, a point about half-way and convenient to both him and his date.

"You've got to be flexible," his niece said.

He said he would be and she wished him good luck.

He phoned Saturday at two o'clock to firm up details and mentioned the Indian restaurant. The hollow line lingered on for several seconds.

To break the silence, he asked, "Is Indian food too spicy?"

"No. I just don't want to drive near the Strip at night."

He understood. Over the years Las Vegas had turned into a city with all of a city's problems, especially negotiating traffic at night. This called for flexibility. "Okay, make a suggestion."

She picked an Italian restaurant in Henderson's Green Valley, a half hour or more by freeway.

"Fine," he said, "If I head out at five-forty-five, I can beat the traffic and meet you by around quarter past six."

"Oh, no. I can't. Let's make it seven."

He felt a tightening of the lateral muscles in his neck. "Okay, seven. I'll call for reservations." He jotted down the name of the restaurant, said goodbye, and opened the yellow pages.

As he dressed, he tried to avoid noticing Darlene's picture on the dresser, but he couldn't. The eyes seemed to follow him no matter where he moved in the bedroom. What had been on his wife's mind the moment the shutter snapped? Sometimes it seemed she must have been struggling to recall some lost fact that lay hidden in her mind. Other times she seemed more or less contemplative, the way she'd look when assembling a jigsaw puzzle. She'd loved puzzles, any kind. And he'd enjoyed watching her assemble them, her face placid, almost regal. She'd picked up the pastime of playing puzzles from her grandfather, an Episcopal priest, who'd relax in the evening by smoking a pipe while thumbing the pieces into place.

He buttoned the last button on his shirt, tucked it in, and walked to the dresser where he held Darlene's picture at arm's length. He sighed and set it face down on the dresser. *Four years*, he thought. He studied the ties on the rack in the closet. Details had counted to her, and Darlene had made them matter to him. He'd surrendered most choices to her because she was invariably right and took delight in preparing for a night out, dining and attending a concert or a show on the Strip. She'd believed the loss of decorum had begun with his and her generation and was on an ever-deepening decline. She'd deplored the jeans-and-tee-shirt culture that had come to infest Las Vegas nightlife, and whenever they'd gone out on the town, she'd insisted on appropriate dress—tie and evening dress, shawl in cool weather, open shoulders on warm evenings, blue tie to compliment his eyes, burgundy to go with his tan coat. He ran a hand down a silk tie, feeling the smoothness of the thread as she had before pecking him on the lips and checking the knot, always a Windsor.

No tie, he decided. Jeans and open collar. He slipped off the dress shirt and trousers he'd put on and changed into a pair of jeans and a polo shirt. Then he put on his houndstooth sport jacket and looked at his image in the mirror. Darlene would never approve, but times had changed and so would he.

Two minutes later he was backing out of the driveway and wondering why he was willing to drive twenty-five miles in Saturday night traffic to meet a stranger, a woman he'd connected with through an online dating service. It couldn't be him doing this. But it was. What were the statistics? One in four relationships now start online. He wondered if she had tattoos.

He followed Mona's directions from memory, but found, just as he'd experienced in the past, that the streets of Green Valley were poorly marked. He missed the critical left turn because he saw the street sign too late to shift lanes. He righted matters, making a U-turn at the next major intersection, but still arrived at eight past seven. The front parking lot was packed. He found a space in the rear and hurried to the restaurant entrance where he gave his name to the hostess, a young woman with a pleasant and well-practiced smile and a clipboard in hand. People waiting for tables were packed around the foyer. He asked if the other person in his party had arrived. The hostess shook her head and said, "If you wish, you can have a drink and wait in the bar."

"That's okay. I'll sit over there." He took a seat facing the door.

Five minutes later, a second hostess, a near-clone of the first, approached and told him his date had been there and left.

"Really."

"Yes. She said she'd forgotten her phone."

"Her phone?" He found the idea of it unsettling.

"Yes."

"I see," he said. *Be flexible*, he thought.

Five more minutes passed. He was hungry and his patience was waning. He was considering leaving when he looked toward the door and saw a woman weaving her way toward him. It was her, but not quite. As she neared, he realized the photo he'd admired was dated. Ten years or more. Though older in life than her photo suggested, she was still attractive and well dressed.

"Hi, Les. At last," she said and extended her hand.

He stood and took her hand. "Yes, nice to finally meet you."

"Sorry. I need my phone." She clutched it like an extra heart or some other organ vital to her survival.

He told the hostess that his party was here. The young woman smiled and said she'd had to give the table to another pair, that it would be a while. Perhaps they'd like to wait in the bar.

He asked Mona what she'd like. Wine. That was fine with him. She left it to him to select from the list. He ordered two glasses of Syrah, a wine Darlene had been fond of. Mona's phone buzzed. She looked at the text window, shook her head and said, "Not important."

The bar crowd was loud, especially the four young women seated at a high-top table directly behind them. It was difficult to hear and although Mona talked freely, not much of what she said registered. From Texas. Austin. Worked for a while at PBS. For a time at the University of Texas. She was a "Hook 'em Horns girl," she said proudly. Then something about taking the job while her ex-husband was gone. *Gone where?* he wondered and was going to ask but didn't. The level of noise dropped considerably. He looked over his shoulder and saw that the young women were filing out.

Shortly after, the hostess came in and said their table was ready. They followed her into the restaurant. At a table for two in the second row, she set the menus down and started to speak.

Mona shook her head. "This won't do. We'll wait for a booth by the window, if that's okay?"

The hostess smiled and said that a party was getting ready to leave. It would be a few minutes, maybe fifteen. "The view's really nice from there," Mona said.

The windows faced the eastern side of the valley where houses and malls and businesses sprawled to the foothills and the mass of lights receded into a gelatinous glow. "Fine," he said, but the thought crossed his mind that the view wouldn't have mattered to Darlene.

Any table, if the two of them were seated together, would provide all the view they needed.

They returned to the waiting area, where Mona talked about how she came to host a radio show. It seemed she'd been a writer for the show and when one day the regular host couldn't do the show, she stepped in and shortly thereafter it became her gig. She smiled, one of those smiles that suggests a response is required. He didn't know what to say. Should he congratulate her on a long-past accomplishment? He asked how long she'd kept the show going.

"Three years. Then I went to Germany to join my husband."

"I see."

The hostess returned and said a window table was waiting. They followed her. When they reached the booth, Mona looked at the table across the aisle where the same four young women were seated, each with gift bag in front of her. They were celebrating someone's birthday. Mona placed her hand to her lips and shook her head.

"That one's empty," she said and pointed to the third booth away.

"It hasn't been cleared," the hostess said.

"We'll wait," Mona said. She looked at him. "You don't mind, do you?"

Les said it was fine. The hostess, her calm expression masking whatever was churning in her head, said, "It'll be a moment. If you wish, you can wait in the bar again."

Mona said, "We'll wait here," indicating the area meant as a bussing station.

Blood flowed to his cheeks. He looked at his wine glass, barely touched, then at the carpet, then at the city lights glowing outside the window. Waiters and waitresses, swinging trays to the side and switching paths for one another, hurried by. They had to sidestep Mona and Les, and he was embarrassed for himself and the staff. Mona, seemingly oblivious to the inconvenience they were causing the help, told of an episode in Germany when her husband was in an accident on the autobahn.

"He was doing over a hundred and was rear-ended. Now, imagine. A hundred. Most people get rear-ended when they're stopped."

"Was he injured badly?"

"Excuse me," a server said as she swiveled her tray to the side in order to pass.

"Are we ever going to get a table?" Mona muttered.

"Was he?"

"What?"

"Hurt."

"Not Mr. Teflon."

The bus help cleared off the table and the hostess swirled into view as if conjured from a Byzantine lamp. "It's ready."

As they settled into the booth, the waitress arrived. Smiling pleasantly, she reeled off the night's specials. He ordered from the menu—chicken Parmesan. Mona selected the second special on the list—giant scallops in wine sauce served over linguini with sun-dried tomatoes. By then it was eight o'clock. He'd had a pita sandwich just before noon. He was famished.

"Was married ten years," she said. "He was my high-school sweetheart and brilliant. My parents disapproved of him, but we were determined. He joined the air force. That kind of set our marriage up for failure."

She let the comment hang, so he asked, "What kind of failure?"

"Oh, being an officer's wife came with all sorts of requirements. You know, having lunch with the other officers' wives and deferring all the time to the wife of the ranking officer. And he was gone. I missed home."

She went on to explain their having had a son added to the problems, because she became the sole caregiver. He listened, but as he did he wondered if a former marriage was appropriate subject matter to pass across the table on a first date. Should he feel free to talk about the physicians telling Darlene and him that children were out of the question, that they should consider adopting? Should he say that Darlene's children became her students at the college where she taught computer science classes?

The son from her marriage, Mona said, was an exceptional athlete, tall and quick, a football star whose knee was injured. She named him, but the name didn't register with Les. The boy later took up golf and wanted to be a pro, the kind who competed on the circuit, but instead he taught at country clubs. He was married now, had two children, and had moved to Maryland. As Mona spoke of her son's accomplishments, the hostess seated a large party of mostly young women, tall and leggy, accompanied by a man and woman in their late forties. Mona seemed distracted by them. Two more young women joined the party. The others stood and embraced them. Les wondered what the occasion was.

Mona leaned across the table and said, "There goes the quiet conversation."

The meal came. The proportions were large and the presentation fine. He sized up his food and figured that under normal circumstances he could never eat it in a single sitting, but it was half past eight and he felt as if his stomach could accommodate a crop of wheat and a cow or two. He sliced into the chicken, cutting off a modest bite. Mona forked a scallop and bit into it.

He swallowed his chicken. "Very good," he said. "You picked a good place."

She nodded, then raked her fork through the linguini, looked across at him and drew her face into a frown.

"Is something wrong with yours?" he asked.

"There's only two tomatoes in mine," she said. "It said with sun-dried tomatoes."

Her words sounded like an indictment.

As the waitress passed by, Mona signaled her to stop. "This won't do. I need more tomatoes."

The waitress looked at the plate and said, "I can take it back."

"No, just bring me some on the side."

The waitress apologized, said she would take care of it, and scurried off. The older woman at the table across the aisle raised a wine glass and proposed a toast. The gathering clinked their glasses, took sips and cheered. The waitress returned with a bowl of sun-dried tomatoes. Mona thanked her and ordered another glass of wine. The waitress said she'd be back shortly with the wine.

"Did that bother you? Asking for more tomatoes?"

He smiled. "No." But it did.

Mona picked up the conversation about her son for a time, then her ex-husband, who'd remarried. She never remarried, though she'd been engaged twice, "But those stories," she said, "are too long to tell." She shifted her conversation to her mother and father who'd divorced when she was seven. She and her brothers went with the mother and had remained estranged from their father up to the time of his impending death. The father had been an investigator at one point, then a successful stock analyst who died wealthy. He'd willed all the money to his second wife. The money didn't concern Mona's mother, who inherited a substantial sum from her own family, but Mona and the sons felt betrayed.

He ate and listened. The wine arrived. The waitress asked if everything was all right. He nodded. The party next to them was sustaining several conversations at once. He noticed for the first time the music playing in the background, Barbra Streisand singing, "The Way We Were." He remembered the story one of his colleagues at the college had told him about her insisting on having fresh rose petals in her toilet bowl at all times. He'd told the anecdote to Darlene, who'd found it amusing.

"Did you know," he said, "that Barbra Streisand demanded rose petals be in her toilet at all times?"

"Is this a joke?" Mona asked.

"No. But it does make you wonder if someone had to be on standby whenever she flushed. You know, just to—"

"That's not good dinner conversation."

"No," he said. "Guess it's not."

He went about devouring the rest of his meal as Mona expanded on her family tale. She finished half her linguini and set the plate aside.

"Now my mother has Alzheimer's. And she's cut us all out of her will, except my older brother who's never been a bit of help. She wants to leave the rest of her money to a community theater in Palm Springs. I quit a job and dropped everything for three years to take care of her."

"That's a lot to sacrifice." He remembered as the end neared how he'd wanted to take family leave and devote time to Darlene, but she insisted he keep teaching his classes, that his students had signed up to have him especially. He owed it to them to be their teacher.

"You don't know what it's like until you have to deal with someone who's sick that way," Mona said. "They're helpless one minute and the next, who knows?"

He pictured Darlene after the third chemotherapy treatment, the one that sparked the beginning of hair loss—at first strands, then clumps. She'd sit bent over the table, penciling in a word or examining the piece of a puzzle, and finger out clusters of hair that she'd toss in a wastebasket. Once she'd gone bald, she refused to wear a wig and instead wore scarfs. He'd wanted her to say that none of it was fair because that was how he'd felt. She was forty-four at the time and he was fifty-four. It should have been him.

The waitress stopped at their table to ask if everything was satisfactory. Mona pointed to her half-eaten meal. "I'll need a to-go box."

The waitress asked if they wanted to see the dessert menu. Mona said yes. Les thanked the waitress for asking and declined. When the waitress arrived with the to-go box, Mona ordered tiramisu. Les was amazed at the size of the dessert, at least six inches square. The waitress brought two spoons. She set one before him and placed the dish between them.

"Eat some," Mona said.

"I'm full. You go ahead."

"I'll never," she said.

"Well, take the rest home."

She took a bite. "It's wonderful."

He watched her eat as she unraveled the rest of her family tale, finishing with why she was in Las Vegas and not with her eighty-four-year-old mother.

"When my back was turned, she attacked me. Tried to choke me."

"What did you do?"

"Nothing. It came out of the blue. She left bruises on my throat."

"No, I meant, what did you do afterward?"

"I left. My brothers can take care of her now."

Five minutes later the tiramisu had disappeared.

"That was great," she said. "I shouldn't have finished it. I'll feel the consequences. I have to go to the ladies' room. I'll be back."

He watched her wind her way around the aisles and felt an easing of the muscles in his neck and back. He hadn't been aware of their stiffening up. He looked at the nearby table and noticed how all of the young women were dressed in evening attire, mid-thigh skirts and heels, and the woman whom Les assumed to be the wife wore a silk evening gown. The man was filling wine glasses around the table. The young women, their faces alight with joy, were chatting and smiling and motioning wildly with their hands.

He swirled the last bit of wine that remained in his glass and listened over the noise to the piped-in music. He remembered their last meal out. He'd bought Darlene a new gown because by then all her clothes hung on her. After she'd dressed, she tried on a dozen scarfs before deciding that the first one was the best, then she insisted on picking out a tie for him. A cane for support on one side, him holding her other arm, they'd gone to the closet, where she selected a red and blue tie and told him to wear his blue blazer. She was so frail by then that he'd tried to talk her out of going, but she was determined. That night, over a meal at Le Vin Rosé, she told him that she wanted him to find someone else, that he shouldn't spend his remaining years alone.

"Are you ready?"

He looked up and saw Mona standing over the table, in her hand the to-go box. How long she'd been there he didn't know. "Yes."

As they walked to the exit, Mona seemed subdued. He remained reticent. *How,* he wondered, *had it been so easy? The emails? The phone conversations?* Now he had nothing to say and it seemed she'd exhausted herself of words. He opened the door. Silence and the chill night air, dry and soothing, greeted them.

"I'll walk you to your car," he said.

She pointed to the west. He walked beside her, neither of them talking. The car wasn't a car, but a black Range Rover, her mother's vehicle she explained and now hers to use because her mother could no longer drive. He nodded. She waited.

He took her hand, squeezed it gently and let go. "I'll call," he said, but it was a lie and he figured she sensed his true intention.

When he reached his car, he turned on the engine and sat looking at the glowing light in window of the restaurant. Another couple was seated where he and Mona had been. The sprawling city lay framed in the rearview mirror, a view that had changed rapidly in so few years. But he hadn't. Now he wondered if he could, if that was possible, if jeans and a polo shirt made him fit in his new life. The evening had been strange, nothing like he'd expected, but now sitting in his car and closed off from the sounds of the world, his judging Mona seemed somehow wrong. Maybe she needed to talk. Loneliness does that. What concerned him was that he hadn't talked, not in the sense of revealing anything of himself. In two years, he'd be sixty. A man of that age should have something to reveal. But how does a man talk about his having been happy most of his life when others measure theirs by their unhappiness?

Darlene might have scolded him for lying. She'd hated lies as much as she loved the precision of math and the logic of computers. She would understand, certainly. At least that's what he hoped. She invariably knew what was right for everyone. That last week she'd insisted on going to hospice care. She didn't want his "last memory of her to be a corpse in their bedroom." She wanted him to remember her as she'd been in graduate school where they'd met in 1984, the same year Kristine Holderied became the first midshipman at the U.S. Naval Academy and Katherine Sullivan became the first woman to walk in space, for her the year women broke forbidden barriers and saw they could be anything they wanted to, including the wife of a man ten years older who didn't know how to dress for an evening out and who read novels and wanted to teach literature and wanted to spend the rest of his years with her. For him it had been his year, the year he'd discovered happiness. No, he couldn't talk about it, not even about the sadness his empty house now brought. It was a sadness that seemed to demand he endure it in silence.

He backed out of the space and ten minutes later was on the freeway following a parade of taillights. "I tried," he said, and repeated it several times before turning into his driveway and walking into his darkened house.

a cop story

I SAT LISTENING, BEER in hand, as my fellow officers recounted their tales. Stories that are more like war stories, not battle stories, but anecdotes that tell of human frailty and humor, stories that test the fuller truth of an experience. I lifted my beer to my lips and stared at my face in the barroom mirror, wondering if I could ever tell anyone the story that hung over me, a story that began in full a little past nine when the call came: "Dead bodies. See a woman at Space 24 in Palm Village Trailer Park."

Bodies, the word landed hard on me. The only thing cops dread more than a family-beef call is a dead-body scene. I'd seen enough dead already. Some haunt you, like the woman standing up over a sink in her underwear as she tried to swallow down some Maalox, but instead coughed up blood and bled to death—forty-three, a cocktail waitress at Caesars Palace. Sad. She died alone, gravity taking charge of what fluids she had left in her, ankles swollen nearly twice their normal size, urine pooled at her feet. That dead body.

The last thing I needed was another dead body. I was, after all, burdened with my own problems. In the middle of the night two weeks earlier Collette had shaken me awake. She stood at the side of the bed looking down, her bottom lip trembling, no words in her, just the lost expression on her face announcing what was taking place. *Not again*, I thought, *another miscarriage*. She pulled the sheet off the bed and wrapped it around her. I sprang out of bed, gathered her in my arms and carried her to the car where she huddled against the inside of the door and sniffled as blood spread out on the sheet. Cursing our bad luck, I ran to the driver's door. As I started the engine, she looked away from me and said, "Hurry, hurry."

This fetus she'd carried for nearly five months, one month longer than the others. She'd seen its dolphin-like image on a sonogram, had listened to its faint heartbeat, had written down a list of boy's names, bought him his first baby clothes and had begun to feel the deep connection of mother to child. Though I tried to reassure her as we drove to the hospital, I knew my words were being sucked into the void that had, after four miscarriages, left us all but estranged. When she finally looked in my direction it was to tell me to shut up. And I did.

Then, the day before I got called to the trailer park, a stranger had knocked on the front door. He'd said, "You're served," and handed me papers. Divorce. After four years. I called Collette at work. She said she just couldn't take it anymore.

"Take what?" I asked. "Me or bringing my work home?"

"Neither."

"What then?"

She said that I didn't know what love was, that I couldn't understand what she was going through, that she wanted, no, *needed* a child. When she said that, I realized the truth was that maybe I didn't know how to love or that I'd forgotten how to. What I did know with some certainty was that I didn't show her love often enough, not because anything was wrong with Collette. Fact was, she was smart, attractive, fine in every way. Guys at the cop shop ribbed me, said she could've done better. They didn't know how true their little joke was. I knew, of course, that the miscarriages hung over our marriage.

"I can't have babies with you," she said.

"What?"

"You heard me."

"That's no reason for a divorce. I mean, we can adopt. We can have a dog."

"A dog? What's wrong with you? The doctor said it may be because of genetics or maybe because of a build-up of antibodies . . . He said it may be you, your sperm, that maybe yours isn't compatible with me. With my egg."

"Maybe there's a solution to that."

"I've found one," she said and hung up on me.

That evening when I came home, she was seated on the couch, a magazine open on her lap. She looked up and said, "I'm sorry. I should've warned you about the summons, but my attorney told me not to."

We stared at one another in a way that suggested we both knew it was futile. She told me it was best that I find an apartment. I was angry and told her maybe she ought to find one instead. She said, "Take it up with an attorney."

It was the nearest we ever came to a real fight. I knew my faults as well as she did. My feelings for her ran deeper than how she perceived them. I didn't always know how or when to express them. Sometimes I came off as a jerk. The next morning, I dressed in my uniform. I needed work to take the mess away.

I TURNED RIGHT OFF Tropicana and passed through the trailer park entrance. I steered left on the third street and stopped at the address. I threw open the car door and immediately smelled death in the air. Across the pavement a gray-haired woman in a robe and slippers hailed me.

"In there," she said, pointing to the trailer. "I've got a key."

I took out my notepad and pen. "Your name."

"Ann. Annabelle, actually. Last name Newman, spelled like Alfred P."

"What?"

"Mad Magazine. Alfred," she said.

"Never read it."

"N-e-w-m-a-n."

"Got it. Tell me what you know."

She explained that she'd known the couple for several years, Donna and Timothy Sands, nice people, heavy drinkers, especially the husband. She said they were quiet, said they waved at her all the time and trusted her enough to give her a key so that she could feed their dog when they went out of town. They had children in California. She said that she smelled the stink coming from the trailer for two days, but she waited one more day before knocking on the door. She got no answer. Inside, she heard their dog whimpering. She unlocked the door.

"I nearly retched from the smell. They were on the floor. I stepped in just enough to make sure. You know, just a step or two."

"Anything else?"

"The dog had eaten at them."

She said that she didn't want to go near the trailer again, that she was even thinking about moving. She stretched her hand toward mine and dangled the key in the very tips of her fingers as if she were holding a scorpion by its stinger.

"I rent here. I don't own," she said, letting go of the key. "He ate them."

I went to the patrol car, opened my briefcase and took out a jar of Mentholatum and a packet of cotton I keep for such moments. I rolled two tight cotton balls, dipped them in the oily rub and jammed them up my nostrils. Detectives would arrive soon, as would someone from the coroner's office. My job was to take notes and preserve the scene. Simple. The door to the double-wide swung open easily. It was dim inside, curtains drawn on all the windows. A sliding glass door led to a porch on the west side. I stepped inside.

I saw no blood anywhere, dried or otherwise, or any signs of a violent struggle. On the floor at the entry to the kitchen, half on the linoleum and half on the carpet, the three of them lay, a man, a woman, he on his back, she on her side, arm resting over his chest, an uncapped bottle of vodka between them. Close by, his paws extended between their heads, lay a fawn-colored boxer, two, maybe three years old. He looked up, his eyes confused and curious. He whimpered and slowly lowered his jowls onto his paws and gazed at me.

Despite the menthol, the stench was more than I could bear. Based on the scene, I pieced the events together. The man likely died of some natural cause. Heart attack. Stroke. Ruptured spleen. Who knew? He was in his seventies, rail thin. His wife, roughly the same age, had lain down, possibly to comfort him, perhaps not realizing he was already dead. Then she, with the help of the vodka, joined him. Anthony and Cleopatra, they weren't, but it was that same tale. No asp, just booze.

I studied the marks on the bodies long enough to surmise that the dog hadn't tried to eat them as the Newman woman had said. It seemed instead that he'd scratched at them and left scrapes on their swollen flesh. I called the dispatcher and asked her to roll an animal-control unit, then radioed my sergeant and told him the deaths appeared natural. From then, my job was to turn, leave, close the door, secure the trailer.

The dog lifted its head and whimpered again. His ribs protruded as he breathed in.

"What's your name?" I asked.

He released what seemed a sigh of resignation. It reminded me of a sad refrain coming from a blues guitar. Then his eyes, brown and pleading, gazed at me and said what words never could. Though it violated procedure, I walked around the bodies. A box of dog biscuits sat on the kitchen counter, too high and far back for the dog to get to. I took a treat out and held it close to his nose. He sniffed it, but made no effort to take it.

"Have it your way, then." I stepped around the bodies and went to the door.

He released that mournful sound again. I turned back, kneeled and held the treat out in my open palm. "Come'ere, boy," I said gently. "Good dog. Come."

He didn't budge.

"Come!" I said in my sternest cop voice.

He'd gone for several days without water and struggled to get to his feet, took two steps and collapsed. I called again, sternly. He tried crawling, but didn't have the strength to maneuver around the bodies. I pocketed the biscuit and walked back. He looked up, eyes expectant, but wary. I picked him up. He trembled in my arms, but didn't resist. I carried him to the living room, laid him on the carpet and broke the biscuit into small pieces. He wouldn't take it. I pried open his jaw and stuck a crumb in. He spat it out. I forced the same piece back in.

"Come on, buddy, eat."

Gradually he chewed and swallowed it.

"Good dog."

I petted his flat head and for another few minutes kept feeding those bits to him. I did so until he ate the entire biscuit, all the while lying down, his paws outstretched. I went to the kitchen and got another. I heard the detective unit pull up, stuffed the treat in my pocket and hurried to the dog. Still trembling, he tried to stand, but his hind legs splayed out as if he'd slipped on ice. I carried him out, just as the detectives stepped from their unit.

"What's this?" Marvin Hicks asked, pointing to the dog.

I shook my head. "He couldn't walk."

"You couldn't wait for animal control?"

"Figured he'd be in the way."

Curt Leavette walked up the driveway and stood beside Hicks. "What we got?"

"Two dead. Bodies are inside," I said.

They shuffled past me. I carried the dog to the patrol car, opened the door and sat with my feet on the hardtop, the dog propped in a sitting position between my ankles. The Newman woman came out of her trailer and crossed the road.

"You've got Charlie," she said. "He looks bad."

"He needs water."

She turned and hurried back to her trailer.

"Charlie, huh?" I petted him on the head. He looked down. "Yeah, that fits."

The woman returned with a bowl of water and set it in front of Charlie. "I can't believe he'd do that," she said.

"Do what?"

"You know, eat them."

"Oh, no. Don't think that. He didn't. Those were scratches. He probably tried to wake them up."

I lifted him to his feet and supported him so that he could drink. He looked back at me.

"Go ahead, boy," I said.

He sniffed the water, then took a tentative lap from it. That seemed to stimulate him to stand on his own. After lapping up a good portion of the water, he quit trembling.

The coroner arrived and the animal-control officer pulled in behind him. The Newman woman excused herself, gathered up her bowl and left us. I aimed my thumb in the direction of the trailer. The coroner nodded and went to the door. The animal-control officer was in her mid-thirties, thin and athletic. I'd never seen her before. She smiled as she neared us. Her hair was tied in a modest ponytail, her eyebrows neatly plucked, eyelashes thick and barely touched with mascara.

"He looks bad," she said kneeling down in front of Charlie.

I petted him and said, "His name's Charlie."

She studied him. "Can he walk?"

"I had to carry him out here."

"From the look of him, he's not likely to make it. I've seen them euthanized when they looked better."

Without giving it a thought, I said, "Not Charlie. He'll make it." I rubbed my palm over his smooth flat skull. "Won't you, buddy?"

"Well, it's not our decision," she said. "I'll bring a cage over and put him in it."

"Charlie," I said, "it's been sweet, but you're on your own now. I've got work to do."

I had to make him see me, see a friend before he was caged and taken away to who knows what fate. I kneeled in front of him and cupped his jowls in my hands. Maybe if I hadn't looked in his eyes and noticed how trusting they were, I could have left matters at that. But I saw in him the very emptiness I was feeling.

The animal-control officer returned with the cage. "Let's go, boy," she said. "Say goodbye to your friend." She clutched him around the chest and started to nudge him into the cage.

"Excuse me," I said. "What's your name?"

"Officer Hendrix."

"Do me a favor, Officer Hendrix."

"Kathleen," she said.

"Kathleen. Let me carry him over."

She looked around as if looking to see who might be watching us. "I guess that's okay."

After Charlie was locked away, I took a business card out of my shirt pocket and handed it to her. "Give this card to whoever does the intake on him. Tell them not to do anything with him until I come by. If there's expense involved, I'll take care of it."

She looked at me, her face all business. "You know what you're saying?"

"Yes."

"I'll be taking him to a shelter. The staff and maybe a veterinarian will look at him. They make the determination. Besides, as I said, from the look of him, keeping him alive's going to be, well, a challenge."

"I think he's up to it. So am I. Look, I'm sure you can pull strings somewhere."

"I'll try."

That afternoon, as I entered the debriefing room, my sergeant gave me a message that I was to call a Kathleen Hendrix. "You got a girl on the side?" he asked and winked.

"It's business."

I called the number and she said that Charlie was at the Lied Animal Shelter and that a woman on the staff named Grace was expecting me to come by. I did. First, I stopped at a pet supply store and bought a box of smoked jerky.

His condition much the same, Charlie lay on his side in a cage. Grace told me he was dehydrated and malnourished and needed fluids, that a volunteer vet was called and on her way to put him on an IV. He lifted his head when he heard me call his name.

"Can I give him this." I showed Grace the strip of jerky.

"You can try. We give them dry food. You can see his bowl is untouched. He did drink some water."

She opened the cage and I went in. Charlie's ears perked up. I held the jerky to his nose. He sniffed it. His stubby tail moved tentatively from side to side. I broke off a piece. He took it and chewed. I broke off another, and then another, until it was gone. Grace waited patiently outside.

"It looks like you two have a connection," she said.

"Charlie and me," I said, "this week dropped a lot on us." I handed her a second piece of jerky and told her to take care of him, that I had plans for Charlie.

Charlie did get better. For a time.

I'd like to say that he survived and that I took him home and we shared many happy years, long walks, me feeding him treats at the dinner table, him chasing a ball, me throwing it, but that would make our story a fairytale and it's not. I returned every day for a week, was gone from the house so often that Collette thought I had moved out and accused me of taking a mistress. Instead of telling her what I was really doing, I told her that I wished I had both moved out and taken a lover. I reminded her that nothing about the division of property had been settled and it was still my house.

Whenever Charlie heard my voice, he'd struggle to his feet. Seeing him do that gave me a moment of joy. I gave him treats and I told him what a good dog he was and how I knew he'd come through this because he had character. Then I would sit beside him and talk, tell him how we'd agreed on who got what property, how Collette was packing up dishes to move, that she was taking the new TV and leaving me the old one, that I'd have the house but it would be empty, and I'd tell him that he had to get better.

The last day I came home after seeing him, Collette asked, "Where exactly are you going after work? What the hell are you up to?"

"I don't know," I said. "Does it matter?"

"You're a great communicator. Do you have any feelings?"

"I do. I wanted a baby too. Maybe not the way you do or for the same reasons."

The shelter called the next day. Collette was in the bathroom opening and closing drawers as she boxed up what she'd be needing in her new place. She answered the phone and said that a woman was on the line asking for me. I picked up the hallway extension and said hello. It was Grace. I told her to hold on and waited until Collette had cradled the extension.

I knew why Grace had called, but said, "Go ahead."

"I'm sorry to bring the news, but I figured you'd want to know."

I thanked her, hung up the phone, and stood in front of the hallway mirror as I struggled to keep my emotions in check.

Collette hollered, "What was that call about? Is that why you haven't been coming home after work? You could've waited a while."

I walked to the bedroom that we once shared and said, "The call was about Charlie."

She slipped a bag full of cosmetics to the side and turned to me. "Who's Charlie?"

"A pal."

"See? That's what's wrong with you. I ask a question and you evade the answer!"

I whispered, "I know."

They said Charlie died from malnutrition. I knew better. Charlie died of a broken heart. I think of him and his feeble effort at wagging his stub of a tail, his struggle just to chew a treat or lap water from a bowl. And I think of a woman lying down beside her dead husband and letting her life drift away, their dog beside them waiting for them to awaken from that forever sleep. I know, as Charlie taught me, that love is about heartbreak, not at first, but in time. But first there is love.

How do you tell that to a bunch of cops in a bar when they're laughing about the story of a prostitute who used a chair to beat up her pimp? How do you swallow a shot of tequila and talk about the empty chair across from you at the table at dinner? How do you tell

43

them about your longing to watch her stir awake? Or just lay her hand on the back of yours? How do you tell them she left you because she believed you couldn't give her the baby she wanted? How do you tell them that the only one who ever heard that story was a dog? You don't. Instead, you tell them a cop story, the one about the guy who tried to commit suicide on his front lawn with a BB gun and broke off a front tooth.

the boy who smelled colors

Christopher steps out of his VW and takes in the day. It's hot, maybe a hundred and five, the air still, and the desert floor, washed white by midmorning sun, glistens like talc. Above the western peaks, tall clouds sit perched as if weighing themselves until heavy enough to slide into the basin and bring rain. Christopher walks to the passenger side, opens the door for his brother and places a hand on his arm to help him out.

Julian gestures him away. "I can manage." He places his cap on his head, canted to the right, then plants his cane on the ground and sets his feet on the asphalt as if testing for hidden faults. "It's warm," he says.

Christopher hands him a bottle of water. "It's hot. Here, let me." He straightens Julian's hat.

"It's a desert, and, well, hot's a form of warm. If we were on the sun, this would seem cool."

"We're not on the sun and hot's when something is cooking or starting to. I'm starting to cook."

Christopher shades his eyes from the glare of the sun. Only Julian, he thinks, only his odd brother, would choose to visit Arizona in July. "Great idea you had," he says.

"I thought you might like it," Julian says.

"I was being sarcastic."

"I know."

Julian hoists himself from the car seat and turns full-circle as if to soak up the landscape, a ritual Christopher didn't understand until the day Julian explained he needed to feel the air and sun from different angles to experience what the day had to offer. He reaches back and tucks the bottle in his fanny pack. "What direction?"

"This way." Christopher takes Julian's forearm in hand and aims him toward the trailhead. "Careful. There's loose rock."

"I'll be fine. I've got you and this to keep me safe." Julian taps the cane on the ground and takes two steps, his weight supported in part by his cane. "Let's go."

They set out on the trail, Christopher guiding his brother steadily, warning him away from rocks that might cause him to trip. The grade is steep and they move slowly, Julian leaning into Christopher for support. In their boyhood, there were times when Julian would have succumbed to impulse, shaken himself free of Christopher's grip and run madly, his stride akimbo, his arms flailing–a blind boy revolting against his affliction. Occasionally, he'd fall to the ground and sit sprawl-legged, kneading a bruise or blowing air on a scrape. Christopher and he laughed off his misadventures, but their parents took Julian's wounds seriously and punished Christopher for not watching over his younger brother more closely.

"What do you see?" Julian asks.

"Mountains, sage, cactus."

"Are there cliffs?"

"Yep, cliffs, sun, miles of desert. The sky's cloudy to the west."

"It might rain. I can smell it."

A woman and a man walk up trail in their direction. The couple, both in their twenties, slow their pace and move to the far side of the trail. As have countless people over the years, they look at the brothers and smile as if they're now part of some unique event, their witnessing of a sighted man and a blind one together on an adventure. Besides blindness, the other striking difference between the brothers is that Julian, at forty-seven, is pale and nearly as hairless as some newborns. Christopher leads him to the trail side, then steers him forward from behind as he did when guiding him through the stadium at the Sky Socks' games. People stared at them as they passed, on their faces the question of why a blind boy would come to a baseball game, a reaction that at first embarrassed Christopher, but one he eventually embraced. He pictures Julian in the bleachers beside him, listening to pitches snap in a catcher's mitt and uninhibitedly shouting out a strike or a ball based on the sound of the ball landing in the pocket of the glove. He determined hits and grounders in a similar manner.

The woman says, "Nice day."

"Yes," Julian says. "Smells like an amber day. See how the sun lies on the cliffs."

She casts a gaze toward the eastern peaks, still bathed in sunlight, then at Julian's sunglasses and cane. She seems confused. Christopher smiles and nudges his brother forward, neither speaking until the couple's out of hearing range.

"What did they look like?"

"Young. Happy."

"Were they bronzed?"

Christopher, faced with another of Julian's random questions. asks, "Why's that important?"

"People who hike on days like this bronze their skin."

"At least you asked me and not them. Let's go see your desert."

"It's not mine. First time I've visited one, intentionally, I mean. It's supposed to be one of the great deserts."

"I'm glad you didn't pick the Sahara."

"You know some Bible prophets wandered the desert seeking sapience."

Sapience? Christopher's reminded, as he often is, that even if Julian can't see and never could, he devoted years to reading Plato, Sartre and Schopenhauer in braille and earned a master's in philosophy from the University of California, and that his mind was always too active for the family to keep pace with. He pulls down the bill of Julian's cap and says. "Good for them."

Julian straightens the bill. "It means wisdom."

"I know what it means."

A half mile later the land slopes steeply downward. Going down is difficult for Julian, but he soldiers forward unperturbed by his odd slips on loose stones. The trail levels and turns west. A few minutes later they're surrounded by a stand of saguaros. Some rise up twenty feet. Christopher wipes sweat from his forehead with a bandanna. He notices Julian's sweating badly.

"We're here."

He removes his brother's hat and hands him the bandanna.

Julian wipes his forehead and says, "Take me up to one."

Whatever Julian has in mind, Christopher suspects it'll be strange, but that's Julian. He takes the bandanna from Julian and replaces the hat. "Why?"

"I want to stand in its shadow so I can feel how tall it is."

Though reluctant to do it, he guides his brother to the shade side of the nearest giant cactus and stops him about two feet away from it. "We're here."

"Stand beside me."

Christopher steps closer.

Julian fumbles about to find Christopher's shoulder. He lays his palm on it. "Help me feel it."

"The needles look really sharp. One of us might get pricked."

"I trust you. Take my hand," Julian says, holding his arm out parallel with the ground.

"Careful." He takes hold of Julian's wrist.

When they were boys, Christopher was often reckless when caring for Julian and he'd lie about things they did, their wandering through woods above Manitou Springs, Julian plucking leaves and pine needles from branches and smelling them, tasting leaves and asking what color each was. On occasion, Christopher would hide from Julian or let him walk into a tree trunk or tumble down a shallow ditch. Mean things, mostly spontaneous, some intentional. He often resented his younger brother.

Julian extends his index finger. Behind him, angled to the right so he can do as his brother wishes, Christopher carefully directs his brother's fingertip to the furrow between the plant's spiked ribs. The space easily accommodates his finger. Julian slides the tip of his finger up and down twice and says, "It's smooth as skin. It's huge, isn't it?"

Christopher looks up at the heavy handless arms of the cactus aimed skyward as if evincing surprise or surrender. "Yes."

"How tall?"

"Close to twenty feet."

"How much do you think it weighs?"

"I don't know. Tons? It's mostly water."

"Like us," Julian says. The next instant his arm goes limp and he begins to tremble. He grabs at the air to catch his balance.

Christopher pulls him away from the cactus. "You okay? You nearly fell into those thorns?"

Julian licks his lips. His Adam's apple convulses. He takes a few deep breaths and gradually color returns to his cheeks. He swallows and signals for Christopher to let go.

"I said, are you okay?"

Julian nods and sniffs his finger tip, then breathes in deeply. "It's green," he says, "a medium green. It's healthy. It'll outlive us. Or at least me."

"Most cactus are green, and don't be depressing. It's just a plant."

"Nothing is just a plant or an animal or a human or even a rock. I smell sage." Julian offers his hand to Christopher. "Show me."

"Maybe you should just sit a while. It was a tough walk."

"I'm fine."

"Have it your way."

They go to a nearby bush, its leaves parched from summer drought. "In front of you."

"I smell it. I don't need help here."

"Maybe a poisonous snake is coiled in there."

"Funny. Well, wouldn't that give us a story?" Julian chuckles and plucks off a nearly desiccated leaf and sniffs it. "It's waiting for rain. *Artemisia tridentata*, common to the Mountain West, high in camphor content. Native tribes use it as medicine."

"And I needed to know that?"

"Yes, you do. You need to know all I know and then some. You too need a guide."

"Really. So do you. How about we stay here until dark, I leave you and then you can find your way back?"

"Will you leave me with a flashlight."

Christopher, as is often the case, is caught momentarily off-guard by Julian's agile wit. He smiles and says, "Sure. Do you need one with batteries?"

They chuckle at the ongoing banter, both familiar and familial. Still, Christopher's impressed with what Julian knows of esoteric matters. He recalls the previous summer's trip to the French wine regions when another display of Julian's knowledge left him baffled. Julian would hold a tasting glass to his nose, breathe in the aroma and declare, not just the type of wine, but the vintage. He'd speak of citric undertones in a Chenin Blanc or berry flavors in a Haut-Médoc or hold up a glass and describe the depth of a color in a Syrah or the clarity of Chardonnay. At one vineyard in the Rhone region, the vintner said that Julian had the nose and palate of a master sommelier. Christopher knew only that one wine was red and another white, and that he preferred the red.

"Okay, I need to rest," Julian says, offering up his hand for Christopher to take.

Christopher leads him to the side of the trail where two stumpy boulders serve as seats.

"Here. You can sit."

"Thanks," Julian says, but he stands for a time panting before he tells Christopher to help him sit. Christopher eases him onto the boulder. Dwarfed by the desert, they sip water. Julian props the bottle between his knees and uses his cap to swat away a vagrant fly. "You think sage plants were named that because someone thought they were wise?"

"Are we playing the philosopher and pupil game again?"

"It seems wise to have leaves that rest between rains and bloom after a rainfall so they'll smell inviting and draw insects."

They sit in silence for a time, kindling up memories, their versions colored differently, Christopher's mostly tainted by guilt, especially one act in particular. Growing up, Julian got most of the attention from their parents and Christopher sometimes resented it. Occasionally, he'd retaliate by doing cruel things to his brother, the worst being when he went off with some friends and left Julian alone at a mall. Four hours later, Christopher returned to find Julian sitting on a bus bench. Julian had asked, "Why do you hate me?" Thirty-six years later, it pains Christopher to recall the moment.

Julian interrupts the silence. "Do you remember when I started junior high? Mom wasn't home, so you dressed me that first day."

"Yeah, vaguely."

Julian bows his head, looking at the ground as if contemplating it. He turns his face toward Christopher and smiles broadly. "Green suit pants and a red polo shirt and you buckled me up in mother's pink velvet belt."

"I did. One white sock, one blue. One brown shoe and one black. Caught hell from dad for that."

"And I asked you to dress me that way again because I got so much attention."

"And every time I did, I caught hell for it."

"You kept your word and never told them it was my idea." Julian sips from his bottle and sits pensively for a moment before saying, "Eleven years now. I still miss them."

"They were weird, but I guess most parents are."

"Mother, she was unique. She paid for those singing lessons, her thinking because José Feliciano and Stevie Wonder had a special gift, I'd be like them. She was devastated to discover I couldn't carry a tune, but stubborn once an idea got in her head. The violin came next, then the piano. At least the piano wasn't wasted because you took lessons."

"It was wasted on me too. I just learned to read notes and make sound."

"I made sound too."

"None we want to remember."

They sit for a time again without talking, Christopher dreading the subject Julian may bring up, one he's asked him not to mention. It is not a promise of a future.

Julian rubs his thigh and sighs, then says, "Mom wanted me to be a prodigy, wanted me to have some gift to compensate for . . . I think she felt guilty for my blindness. Maybe thought some genetic flaw in her or Dad caused it. Guilt drives people. You ever feel guilty for all the stuff you pulled on me?"

"You've asked me that before." The question cuts into Christopher's guts. "If I did, I'd keep it to myself. You weren't Mr. Perfect. Bet Mom didn't feel very compensated when you doubled up your fists and pounded on the piano keys."

"That *was* pretty terrible."

"It was better than anything else you produced on it."

"Remember when I told her that music wasn't for me."

"Only word for word. We were all eating dinner and you said, "Mom, think how few people, blind or otherwise, are musicians. I don't think music is for me.""

"Yeah, she said I wasn't trying hard enough. I said my real ambition was to be a dancer."

Christopher grins savoring the memory. "Dad spat his lima beans out. We laughed until our sides ached, Dad included. Then Mom got all misty-eyed and said she only wished you could dance."

Julian seems to ponder the memory a moment, then says, "Know what I wanted to be?"

"What's that?"

"The best blind baseball player in the world."

Christopher chuckles. "How could you judge that?"

"Easy. I'd be the only one."

Christopher remembers when he and Donny Lamb would take Julian to the park with them and have batting practice. Julian would take his turn at bat and Donny would crouch behind the plate and Christopher would toss balls to Julian until Julian managed somehow to hit two, always two before they quit. Kids and adults alike would gather to watch. For some it was a freak show, for others a confusing but worthwhile spectacle.

"That would make you the worst as well."

"Okay, then. I really wanted to be the greatest blind artist, deadly with a paintbrush."

A hot breeze blows through a ravine nearby. Christopher gazes west where clouds have crept over the foothills and shaded the wide valley. He figures it's time to go back to the car.

"Seriously," Julian says, "it's not easy to accept what life thrusts on you. It was tough on Mom and Dad. I wore them down. Even you. But we were pals." Julian clears his throat, faces Christopher and seems to gaze at him, his eyes pale and dull, eyes that never saw light or darkness or color. "Maybe that's why I never told Mom or Dad that you left me in the mall. Maybe, because I was protecting them and not you. Or maybe because you were my pal."

"Sometimes, we were pals. Sometimes, I resented you. If you weren't around, I'd . . ."

"You hated me, really?"

"I didn't say hate. Resented, and I'm not bragging about it."

"That's fair. Mom said I'd be able to see when I went to heaven.

She believed that all was better in the spiritual world. Do you believe Mom and Dad's spirits are alive?"

Christopher looks west where clouds have drifted down from the mountains and now sit crouched on the foothills. Yeah, he thinks, alive in our memories. "Julian, I'm not going to talk about that. Remember what I asked? No afterlife, no death. We're on a vacation. No grim stuff."

"They loved you too," Julian says.

"If you say so."

He recalls Julian's ninth birthday, their mother taking pains with the cake and the presents and making certain Julian would have guests, every effort designed to make his brother seem normal. The smell of baked cake in the air was so thick that Christopher couldn't resist the icing. He ran his finger over it, gouging a line through the center of "Happy," and when his mom scolded him, he said, "It's not like he can see." His mom slapped him, the only time she ever did, and said, "Your brother loves you. Be kind."

Julian goes into a sneezing frenzy, clenching his fists and trying to hold back each sneeze. When the episode ends, he lifts his sunglasses from his nose and rubs his eyes.

Christopher uses the bandana to wipe Julian's nose. "Are you okay?"

He nods to himself and sips some water.

"Let's talk about something worth remembering, like the first time you asked me the color of a fruit."

"Was it an orange?"

"No, philosopher. Orange *is* the color of an orange. It was an apple and I told you it was red on the outside and white on the inside."

"Ah, yeah. Then you gave me a green apple and just said it was an apple."

"Uh-huh. You said it couldn't be because it was green. How'd you know?"

"I smell colors."

"Can you smell blue paint?"

"Paint's not alive."

"Answer the question. Can you smell blue paint?"

"Depends. Wet or dry?"

"Wet."

"Yes. It smells like crap." Julian licks his lips and turns his face to the sun. "I can tell the sun's golden by feeling it. And I can smell cancer. It's purple. And black is the color of death. It's the one color I see."

Christopher feels his chest constrict. He can't look at Julian. For the moment, he stares off at the east and the sun-soaked cliffs. In part, it *is* an amber day, the cliffs the colors of rust and autumn leaf. The other part is clouded. He caps the bottle and stands. "We're not discussing it."

"I have to say something," Julian says.

"What now?"

"You were the only one who treated me like I was a person. I mean, you didn't protect me from everything. Because of you, I learned what it felt like to hit a baseball, feeling accompanied sound. Do you realize …" He stops and wrings his hands. "Chris, you let me feel pain and have freedom, didn't act like I was an invalid. Some people see I'm blind and they raise their voices, as if being blind and deaf come as one, or they whisper, thinking the same way. What I'm saying, is that you let me experience the world the way it is. You have to experience it first to understand who you are in it. That's what Epicurus professed. I'm thankful to you for that."

Christopher starts to reach for his brother, but hesitates. They were never an affectionate pair, just as their parents were never openly affectionate. He looks around at the sky, the distant clouds black on the bottom and outlined by a fringe of gray, cliffs amber and shining, then he stands and says, "You ready?"

Julian slips on his sunglasses. "Chris?" he says, the tone of his voice so serious he sounds desperate.

"Yeah? What now?"

"When do I get a crack at driving?"

Christopher walks over to him and tugs the bill of his cap down so that his face is nearly masked.

Julian lifts the bill up. "You were a good chemo partner. Thanks. Can I ask something else?"

"What? You want to touch a prickly pear? Maybe catch a Gila monster or scorpion?"

"This is serious. Will you be okay? You know, if it returns. If it comes out of remission?"

Christopher thinks a moment, considering what his brother is really asking. Does he mean will I miss him? Remember him? He slides the sunglasses down to the brim of Julian's nose, so he can see his brother's eyes. *Love* is a word he uses all the time. He loves coffee in the morning, loves grapes as an afternoon snack, loves reading a good book. He remembers when Julian was six, their parents in the midst of a heated argument in the kitchen. His dad told Christopher to take Julian outside, but as Christopher touched him, Julian pulled away and jammed his index fingers in his ears. "I can make you all disappear. See?" he said. It stunned their parents into silence and the incident became family lore told over the dinner table. *Love*'s too weak a word. He doesn't just love his brother.

"Looks like rain, and it's a long drive. Come on, get up. Lunch will go well."

Julian adjusts the sunglasses. "I've finally visited the Arizona desert. Now the Grand Canyon. And horseback riding."

"Yep. The Grand Canyon."

"And horseback riding. You promised."

"I said maybe."

Christopher helps Julian to his feet, the question hanging between them as they start back on the trail. How do you explain a feeling that goes beyond missing someone? Can it be explained like a ball game or how to swing a bat or what color matches the smell of an apple? Can any word satisfy as an answer? Maybe later he'll tell his brother that, yes, he'll be okay, but just okay. Life will be emptier, much emptier. And he finds the words to describe the feeling fighting to escape his chest and realizes Julian is a gift he'll cherish, and *cherish* is the only word. All others seem weak.

He lays his palm on his brother's shoulder. "Tell me something?"

"What's that?"

"How'd you know the shades of red wine and all that other stuff?"

"A hundred-dollar CD, a few dozen wine classes, and about two thousand dollars invested in wine."

"Cheater."

"I've got a good nose. Next year, we'll go to Argentina, the Mendoza Valley. I've been studying the malbecs. You might find them interesting."

"I probably won't." Christopher claws the car keys out of his pocket, slips them in the palm of Julian's free hand and closes his brother's fingers around them.

"What's this?"

"It's your turn behind the wheel." He wraps his arm around his little brother and pulls him close. *Don't*, he thinks, *don't disappear, don't smell black. Not while I breathe. Smell red and blue and green and feel the sun and describe the day as amber, drink wine with me in Argentina next summer and tell me what the bouquet suggests.*

the day nixon was impeached

My brother Eddie and his friend, Jace, ran a chop shop out of a shed in the Pettibones' backyard. If such a talent is possible, both had perfect pitch for engines. They could hear a car accelerate and identify the engine and components that muscled it. Those were the days of glass-packs and Holly fours, days of protest songs and tripping on acid, days when the public spotlight shined on Nixon's inner circle of goons, and Eddie was my idol.

From transmission to engine to sound system, J & E, as they called themselves, filled orders. Their only overhead was the risk they took in dealing in stolen cars. Eddie was the thief of the enterprise and Jace the chopper half. Pickup jockeys, airmen, shop mechanics and even a cop or two bought their car parts from Jace. On occasion, he'd soup up a stolen car and Eddie would unload it in Juarez, a riskier but more profitable sideline.

So long as Eddie's projects left no oil stains on the patio or in the backyard, our parents overlooked the odd carburetor, gearbox housing, or set of headers lying around. They overlooked the six-month sentence he served in the state reformatory for car theft as well. After all, the state said he was reformed. I read something years later about parents such as ours—absentee parents, overworked and self-absorbed, parents who loved their children but irresponsibly.

Alamogordo was a pretty tough town and Eddie had pulled me out of more than a few scrapes, most recently when Buddy Foster and a kid named Kyle cornered me at the Red Rooster and threatened to beat me up with a bicycle chain. So, when Eddie called the last Tuesday in July and told me to pack some clothes and be ready to stay overnight, I did as told. Shortly after high noon he blew the horn of a red '70 GTO. I grabbed my overnight bag off the couch and hurried out. Eddie, his eyes obscured behind his reflective sunglasses, threw open the driver's door and stepped out.

"Nice wheels," I said.

He nodded. "Yeah, get in the back."

Gloria, his girlfriend of seven months, sat shotgun. I tossed my bag onto the backseat and slid in beside it. He hadn't mentioned Gloria's coming along and I knew better than to ask why, just as I knew better than to ask where he'd gotten the car or where we were headed or his purpose behind our taking the trip. She glanced back as I settled in. Normally, she called me handsome to make me blush.

"Hi, Nicky," she said and looked straight ahead.

I said, "Hi."

Eddie slammed his door and glanced at me through the rearview mirror. "Before you ask, we're going to Mexico."

"I wasn't going to ask."

By Mexico, he meant Juarez. Our previous trips there had been planned in advance and timed so that Eddie could take care of business early enough for us to eat, then cross the border back to El Paso and catch a late bus back home. A last-minute trip was unusual, more so because Gloria was going along. Her mother, Conchita, rode rough herd on her daughters. She'd never approve of one going away overnight with a boy, most especially to a sanctuary for sin like Juarez. But there sat Gloria.

She was what we called a heart-break beauty—dimpled cheeks, Madonna eyes, and shiny dark hair that cascaded to the small of her back. Though she sometimes flirted with me, I didn't kid myself. Unlike Eddie, whose brooding good looks and indifference attracted girls, I was average and mostly shy around girls, but Gloria had a way of making me feel important, and I was at an age where I wanted nothing more than to feel important to someone. I'd developed a fool's crush on her. Everything about her said charm—the sneeze she never quite released and the way she'd fall into a fit of laughter, then cup a hand over her mouth until her laughter subsided. Her laugh was infectious. One look from her would set me off in an episode that left my sides aching. Eddie would shake his head and tell us we were being ridiculous. I pretended those moments of raucous laughter implied a secret intimacy we shared.

"Everybody ready?" Without waiting for our reply, Eddie popped a stick of gum in his mouth and pulled away from the curb.

Gloria looked back at me again. I smiled and waited for her to return it, but she didn't have a smile in her. I assumed Eddie was the cause. She'd been seeing him long enough that I figured this wasn't her first ride in a car he'd stolen, so it had to be something else he'd done or something he'd said.

The day was hot and promised to get hotter and the air conditioning didn't work.

Eddie explained that Jace didn't work on air conditioners yet. "Compressors and refrigeration is somehow beyond him. Besides, he said that he was so cool he didn't need one that worked."

Eddie rolled down the windows, looked at himself in the mirror and ran his fingers through his slicked-back hair. He glanced at Gloria. "You doing okay?"

"Yeah, I'm fine." It seemed she had to wrestle the words out.

"Good. Well, let's all enjoy the ride."

When we reached the southbound highway, Eddie brought the car up to the hated double-nickel speed limit. He liked to speed, but dared not go faster than fifty-five, not while driving in a hot car on a highway crawling with New Mexico state troopers. Hot air poured through the open windows. He flipped on the radio and found a station that played top twenties rock 'n' roll. A newscaster interrupted the music to say that Richard Nixon had been impeached by Congress.

Eddie spat his gum out the window. "Good. Now they should put that crook in jail where he belongs." The newscaster began revisiting the events leading to the impeachment. Eddie said, "We all know what he did," and turned the dial to another station, cranked up the volume and began singing. He nudged Gloria, urging her to sing along. She shook her head and stared out the window.

"That's no way to be," Eddie said. "Just makes things worse."

I thought, *What things? Getting caught in a stolen car? Getting on the bad side of her mother?* I watched sand drift over the dunes that stretched for miles between the highway and the distant mountains. Every once in a while, Eddie would shout above the sound of the wind and radio, asking Gloria if she was okay. She'd nod, but it didn't seem that she was.

Realizing that I hadn't mentioned it, I said, "I left a note for Mom like you told me."

Eddie, intent on Gloria, didn't bother looking at me. "Should I give you a medal?"

"Guess not," I said.

"Leave Nicky alone," Gloria said. "Why do you pick on him?"

Eddie ignored her.

Wild, sometimes cruel, especially with girls, Eddie was generous with me and often kind, unless he was angry, in which case I wisely avoided him. On one trip to Juarez he'd marched me into to El Submarino, a bar on a side street, where he ordered two shots of whiskey. He downed one, then pushed the other in front of me. Trying to emulate him, I swallowed mine and instantly fell to coughing spasms. He'd bent me forward at the waist, slapped my back, and told me I'd be okay as soon as the burning passed. As we walked back to the border crossing, he talked with near reverence about the test of Masai boys my age who carried only a spear and a shield into the Great Rift Valley to kill a lion. He told me that shot of whiskey was my lion and now I was sort of a man, that the real test was a woman and if we had time, he'd treat me to one. The idea of visiting a whorehouse had struck fear in me. Still, I'd told him I was ready. "No, you're not," he'd said, ruffling up my hair.

"I asked why you pick on him," Gloria said.

Eddie smiled at me through the mirror. "Because he lets me."

As on our previous trips, Eddie drove directly onto the international bridge that joined the U.S. and Mexico. He didn't take risks. Of course, little was at stake in crossing the border into Mexico. The risk was in returning to U.S. soil where customs agents in white shirts and black trousers looked for contraband with near-fanatical zeal. I wondered as we neared the crossing if Eddie intended to unload the car or if upon our return, he had a story in mind to explain it.

The Mexican agent signaled us forward, stuck his face in the open window, and grinning, waved us through. We fell in behind a parade of bumper-to-bumper traffic on the Avenida de 16 de Septiembre. The air smelled of leaded gas, smoldering charcoal, and faintly of cured leather.

"Here," Eddie said, "tell me the directions." He handed her a sheet of paper.

She unfolded it and placed it on her lap.

"Well?" Eddie said.

She swallowed and gazed out the window.

"Come on," he said, "read it off to me."

She looked at the map. "Turn left. Two stop lights after the corrida."

We drove past the corrida and the overpowering smell of bovine manure and urine. When I was ten, my father had taken us to the corrida. Mother found it disturbing the way the matador drove a sword deep between the bull's shoulder blades and cut off its ears and tail. She'd claimed the smell of blood was in her hair. Dad had said it was her imagination, that it was good for his sons to be exposed to brutality, that the world was a brutal place and he didn't want us to grow up pretending otherwise. She'd told him to stop talking and the remainder of the drive turned away whenever he spoke. Eddie, seated beside me in the back, had whispered, "You got to envy that kind of love."

"Go straight up this street," Gloria said, "and take the second street right."

Eddie turned left, then took the second right onto a dirt road blemished with potholes, a gauntlet of squat adobe hovels on either side. Fifty feet ahead a boy, maybe four, wearing only shorts, sat in the center of the roadway. The street proved too narrow for Eddie to maneuver around him. He brought the car to a stop and honked. The boy didn't move. Eddie shifted the car into park. Its idling engine rumbled.

"It's a sign," Gloria said.

"A sign? Don't be stupid." Eddie's mirrored shades locked on me as he pressed the horn and held it to the count of three before releasing it.

Gloria said, "Let's go back. I can't. I know I said–"

"Nicky," Eddie said, "go move him." He leaned forward, providing me space enough to climb out of my seat.

Gloria said, "I changed my mind, Eddie. Please, let's just go back."

I hesitated.

"Goddammit, Nicky, get him out of the way."

I squeezed out and approached the boy. He had a stick in his hand and was poking it at a dead mouse. He smiled up at me. I looked back at the car and shrugged. Though the sun's reflection off the windshield obscured my view, I saw Eddie clearly enough to know he was on the verge of blowing up.

He poked his head through the open window. "We don't have all day."

I'd witnessed his rage and knew it best to do as he said. I picked up the boy and carried him to the side. As I sat him down in the shade of a house, he swung at me with his stick. The next instant a woman charged out of the shadows of an adobe hovel and ran toward me, her finger pointing at me as she fired off a string of invectives in Spanish. The neighborhood came alive spontaneously, women and children spilling out onto the road to bear witness. I fled to the waiting GTO. Eddie, in his haste to close the door, nearly slammed it on my foot. Gloria, a rosary looped over her wrist, crumpled the map into a wad and threw it at Eddie, hitting him in the cheek. He caught it before it fell to the floorboard.

I finally asked what I knew better than to ask. "Why're we here?"

Eddie put the car in drive, but kept his foot on the brake pedal. "We're here because she messed up. And you're here because . . . Well, you're here and that's the way it is."

Gloria held the crucifix to her lips, then touched it to her cheek. "Please, let's not. . ." She glanced in my direction, mumbled something, then dropped her hands on her lap.

He pressed on the accelerator and the car lurched forward. The angry mother, now clutching the child to her breasts, jogged beside the car and spat at us as we drove away.

"Turn around, Eddie," Gloria said.

Undaunted, Eddie drove up the block.

Gloria said, "I said turn around. Now."

Eddie hit the brake pedal and brought the car to a stop. A choking dust rose up and formed a cloud around the car. It came through the open windows. I breathed in the dry taste of Mexico and sneezed.

He stared at her. "The map doesn't say turn around."

"Maps don't talk. People do."

"We talked it over and over. Think about your mother, your sisters. Never mind me. That's why we're here."

She stared back. He handed her the wadded paper.

She lowered her eyes and nodded. "Okay then, never mind. Go ahead." She unraveled the crinkled paper, took a breath, and looked at the map. "The next left, one block on the right."

The building consisted of three two-story adobe shops: on one end a *carnicería*, in the middle a *peluquería*, and at the near end a *farmacia*. Above the pharmacy, a small sign mounted next to a cowbell read, "*Comadrona Licenciada*."

"This is it," Eddie said and pulled off the road onto a dirt parking lot.

At the corner, an old man peddled *dulces* out of a street cart. He stared in our direction as we pulled into a parking space outside the pharmacy. The old man crossed himself and looked away. Eddie rolled up his window and told Gloria to do likewise. "They'll steal it if they get a chance," he said.

"Who's they?" she asked.

The irony she intended was lost on Eddie.

He glared at her and unlatched his door. "*They* are anybody here."

She gazed at the stairs that led up to the top floor of the flat-roofed building. Her lower lip quivered. Eddie locked his door, told me to stay in the car and slammed it shut. He walked to her side. As he did, she pressed the door lock. The car was hot-wired. Without a key Eddie couldn't open the door. He pulled angrily at the handle and hollered for her to open it.

"Dammit," he shouted. "Nicky, unlock her door."

When I reached to unlock the door, she pushed my hand away. "Don't," she said, her eyes pleading.

She didn't understand the rule central to my relationship with my older brother—do what he says. I reached again for the latch.

Tears welled up in her eyes. She wiped at them with the back of her hand, said, "Remember this," and lifted the door lock.

Eddie opened the door.

We waited for a time in wordless purgatory. Eddie stood at the door, a hand extended to her. I wondered what would come next. She sat static, knowing. Finally, she shook her head, waved his hand off and set her feet on the ground. He tried slipping his arm around her waist, but she jerked away from him, shook her head and began ascending the stairs. He caught up with her on the landing and rang the cowbell.

A squat Mexican woman opened the door. Eddie passed her a piece of paper. She read it, nodded, and all three disappeared inside. I stared up at the top of the empty staircase wondering how my brother had come to be the way he was—wild, somehow always outside the boundaries. For the better part of three hours I alternately watched for the door on the second-story landing to open and listened to the car radio, rock n' roll and news, most of it about Nixon and Watergate and all the political fallout. As dusk neared, Gloria and my brother descended the same stairs. She leaned against him for support. Eddie carried a paper sack in his other hand. He opened her door, gently helped her sit, came around to the driver's seat and settled in behind the steering wheel.

He parked half a block north of El Submarino, where I'd had my first taste of whiskey.

"I won't be long," he said. He left the two of us and entered the bar.

"Are you okay?" I asked.

"Let's don't talk," she said.

She adjusted her position in the seat, struggling with something at her side. She turned her face at an angle so that I could see nothing but one glistening cheek.

Twenty minutes passed before Eddie reappeared. He nodded to a man approaching on the sidewalk from the opposite direction. The man was older, how much I couldn't tell. He was dressed in jeans and Tony Lama cowboy boots and wore a straw Stetson. The two of them shook hands, then after looking cautiously about, they walked to the next corner and slipped into the shadows. When they stepped out, the man handed something to Eddie, who returned to the car.

Eddie gestured for Gloria to roll down her window, stuck his head inside, and said, "Get ready."

He returned to the man. They exchanged a few words and again shook hands. Then Eddie came back to the car, opened her door and said, "Let's go."

I'd gathered up my overnight bag. He told me to carry the paper sack. Gloria clutched her purse to her abdomen and grimaced as he helped her out. Eddie eased the purse from her hands and slid the strap over her shoulder, then reached down for a small suitcase on the floorboard.

"She's sick," I said. "Can't we just drive across?"

"Don't be stupid." He wrapped an arm around her to prop her up. "It'll get easier as we walk. Come on." He told me to walk on her other side and help if she needed it.

The walk was four short blocks. Even after nightfall, the July heat rose up from the pavement and the milling tourists slowed us. Two blocks from the border my armpits were drenched from both the heat and the tension. I looked at Gloria. Sweat beaded down her forehead. She didn't complain, just kept her eyes on the looming bridge.

Eddie proved right. The farther we went up the Avenida de 16 de Septiembre, the better she seemed. As we neared the bridge, she said she could walk without help. She took a deep breath and straightened her back. "I'll be fine," she said.

"That a girl," Eddie said. "No bus for you. I'll get us a car on the other side, a Cadillac or whatever you want. Nothing's too good for you."

Her mouth turned up in a strained smile. "I hate you, Edward Bowen."

"No, you don't. This is all going to work out."

She reached over and grasped my arm. "Tell him, Nicky. He'll believe you."

Her grasp, weak but desperate, signaled she meant every word. The sun wasn't yet down, but around and behind us flickering street lamps augured the coming night and neon flashed up and down Juarez's main avenue. Ahead, the bridge waited. I noticed a blemish on her chin, red and swollen, a mar on her otherwise flawless skin. She saw me looking, lowered her eyes and turned away. Her shame wasn't over a pimple. I wanted to run back to the GTO, pick her up and drive the two of us across the bridge, crash the gate if need be. But that was all fantasy. I would never be her hero. I realized we were allies, victims of the misadventures that led us here and at the mercy of the moment.

"She does, Eddie," I said. "She hates you."

"What? Well, good," he said. "Keep hating me. I don't care. Now, let's get home."

As we neared the customs checkpoint, my knees trembled. I worried that she wasn't going to hold up or that I'd do or say something stupid. We fell in behind a half-dozen tourist types who quickly passed through customs and walked to the turnstiles, the last barrier to the U.S. An older couple carrying two shopping bags settled behind us. The line grew behind them.

Gloria went first. Her Hispanic bloodline showed in her dark features and olive skin. The customs officer eyed her suspiciously as he asked her nationality.

"U.S. citizen," she said.

"Do you have ID?"

Hands trembling, she opened her purse and took out her driver's license. He studied it a strained moment before handing it back. "What was the nature of your visit?"

"Shopping." She shifted her weight uncomfortably

"What'd you buy?"

She said in a voice thin even for her, "Nothing."

"What's that?"

"Nothing. I bought nothing."

"Put your purse on the table."

She complied and stood staring at her hands. Eddie coughed to get her attention, and in an attempt to steel her against the onslaught of questions, nodded. She didn't acknowledge him. The officer dumped the contents of her purse on the table.

"Nothing to declare. Is that right?"

"Yes."

The man spread the items out, and seeing there was no contraband, pushed her property aside. "Okay, replace them in your purse."

"Next," he said, and asked Eddie's nationality.

"U.S."

The officer told him to place the suitcase on the steel table and open it. "Do you have anything to declare?"

"No."

The man turned the open suitcase toward him, ran his hands under the clothing, turned over a blouse and skirt, both neatly folded, and said, "Looks like you came for a stay. This hers?"

Eddie seemed to be considering a smart-ass answer, but instead nodded.

The guard told him to close the suitcase, then narrowed his eyes on me and the sack I carried. "Citizenship?"

"U.S."

"Your satchel, put it here." He pointed to the table.

I followed his instructions. He unzipped the bag and spread my clothes out, two pairs of underwear, two pairs of socks, and two tee-shirts. Gloria winced and closed her eyes.

"Put those back and set the sack here," he said.

He turned the sack upside down and spilled the contents, half a dozen sanitary napkins. He looked at them as if befuddled. "Okay. All of you step over there." He pointed to where another customs man sat on a stool, talking with a border patrol officer.

The elderly woman standing behind Gloria gasped and said, "She needs help."

The officer looked at Eddie, then down where blood was pooling at Gloria's feet. Before anyone could move to stop her, Gloria lurched forward, collapsed and lay moaning on the floor.

Though she was beyond whatever help we could offer, Eddie and I kneeled beside her. I whispered to him the words I would regret years later, "I hate you too."

He nodded.

IT WOULD BE DISHONEST of me to leave events there, the small ones as well as the big ones. Of course, the attention of the nation had been harnessed for months to the events of Watergate, the many players, and the mystery of Deep Throat. The day Nixon resigned, the populace, fortified by a renewed belief in the system of justice, seemed to breathe a collective sigh.

I spent the night and the next in a juvenile facility in El Paso. Because of my age and because I confessed what I knew, I was spared punishment, but my parents sent me to Nevada to live with my mother's father, a retired lumberjack, and his second wife. Eddie was arrested. He later pled guilty to a misdemeanor offense and agreed to join the service. He died in a dust storm in Iran as part of a crew sent to rescue hostages in the embassy. Gloria, rushed to a hospital that night, didn't die. I heard she eventually married and became a civics and history teacher at Alamogordo High. She never had children.

What happened in the larger world is a matter of history. Nixon resigned, Gerald Ford became president and pardoned Nixon to heal the wounds the nation suffered, then Jimmy Carter replaced Gerald Ford as president, and soon the country was in a fresh crisis, one that took my brother's life. As I lived those years, I wondered what path two small lives might otherwise have taken had a child been born or if a better option were available to Gloria. I don't know if bitterness pursued her in the years that followed or if she managed to somehow forgive, or if not forgive, pardon my brother to heal wounds as Ford had done with Nixon. I like to think she managed to. I know only my own life, how that night in Juarez shaped my path, how I've lived my life without malice for others. I married and had daughters, two of them, and watched over and guided them the best I knew how, and I walked both down the aisle. Occasionally, they resented me for loving them so heedfully, and perhaps I did trespass on their lives too. I wanted them safe from harm. I trust that they will understand my motives when they have children of their own.

sheets

On the third morning since she returned for her clothes, you feel so bad the second beer you gulp down seems to make a turn in the middle of your gullet so you lean over the sink in case it and the tuna sandwich you ate sometime before you passed out come up together. You gag a few times but stave off the vomit. A skillet sits on the stove, the remains of egg stuck under a three-day coat of grease. Alone, you think, with dirty pans and dishes and a dusty cabinet counter is as alone as a man can be. Everything tells you this day will be no different from the last few. It's a goddamn country western song at high volume.

You find it odd how silence can seem louder than noise. Maybe it's just that noise muffles your thoughts. But now in the morning silence, they begin to tighten up like channel locks around your Adam's apple. Your throat constricts, lungs work like you'll never be able to get a deep breath again, no matter what. You turn off the light for a time until dawn breaks on the horizon and blinding sunlight from the front-room window spears into the kitchen. A galaxy of dust motes swirls in the shaft of light above the table where Mr. .357 lies on its side.

You wonder if anger and hate can break a man, not the way your cousin Andy broke horses while leaving their spirited ways intact, but break a man the way dried-out wedding cake crumbles at the touch of a finger and what's left to eat is good only for ants and cockroaches. Cake without moisture is not a good thing. That kind of breaking. But what if anger and hate are all you have, those and an empty house and a bed with no sheets?

The clock reads 6:04 a.m. The dispatcher will be in by now. You decide you may as well call in. You dial the phone and wait.

When Amy Peabody lifts the receiver and says, "Hello," you say, "Peabody, it's me."

"You coming in?" she asks.

"Not today."

"He'll fire you."

"I figure."

"He said another week to get yourself together."

"I been working on it."

"I'll tell him, but don't be surprised."

"Hell, Peabody, I'd welcome a surprise."

"Bye, Bill."

"Yeah, see you."

"Bill?"

"Yeah."

"You okay? I mean, really?"

"Great. Getting on top of it, you might say."

"You won't do something . . ."

"Crazy? No. Bye now."

You hang up the phone and sit at the table plunking shells into the cylinder of your Colt .357, wondering as you do whether to put one in your brain or go after her or go after him or just go after someone. Ain't easy on the head. Even worse on the heart. You thumb the hammer back and lower it a turn at a time and listen hard as the cylinder rotates. The metallic clicks seem to say, "You've been neglecting things long enough. Today, shit heel, get it together."

You look about the kitchen and decide it won't do for a man to go out of the world filthy and leave behind dirty dishes and a floor unswept, so you set the gun aside, heave the empty bottle in the trash, then twist the cap off another and go to work on the mess. Using the spatula, you scrape away the grime on the skillet and sprinkle rock salt on it. You think of the first time you cooked eggs for her, her standing at the kitchen doorway staring at you, her wrapped up in the sheets you burned three weeks ago. Scrambled, she said. Is there another way? you asked. You know better than to wash a skillet, something she didn't know. Took some time to cure, something a woman from Trenton didn't have a clue about when she dumped it in hot suds and scratched the cure off with steel wool. What kind of shit-kicker marries a woman like that? Bill Brady does. Bill Brady, the goddamn fool, does. That kind of shit-kicker. You stir the salt around with the palm of your hand until your palm burns, a pain that feels better than the ache inside you. You scoop the salt out with a paper towel and hang the skillet by its handle on the hook you put up the very day you bought the house. Your house. The house she moved in when you two said I do. Gave up a fine trailer for it.

Hot water and soap, more hot water and even more hot water steams up in the sink. You plunge your hands in it and pull them out, knuckles red as the day you caught them together and laid him out on the bedroom floor, Marie all wrapped up in sheets and embarrassed like you never saw her lady parts before, your wife, her screaming, "Stop, please stop!" But you didn't stop because everything in you said, keep going, him lying on the laminate floor you put down on your own, him sniveling, saying he'd had enough. Enough wasn't enough to satisfy you. You yanked the sheets off her and the next day burned them in the backyard, burned them good, and if you could have, you would have thrown the two of them to the flames as well and plucked your heart out and tossed it on those sheets for good measure, but they were long out of reach of your rage.

Bill, you thought, *you dumb sonofabitch, didn't you know it, didn't you know this was where you were headed when you first saw her?* That's what you thought then. That's what you think now. You hold up a plate and look at your distorted reflection. China. She had to have it. Not any china, fine bone china. The plate's framed in the window. You see the foothills and the distant snow-capped peaks of the Sierra Nevada glistening as the sun rises higher. Over there's where the Donner Party ate each other in order to survive the Sierra winter, and you wonder, *Is life a winter storm and all we do is die slowly in it or eat each other?* And then you glance at the backyard where she planted roses in the holes you dug, where she smiled up at you, happy as a butterfly sucking nectar. Now the bushes are cut back and bare except for some two-day-old snow hanging on them.

You think of your backyard when you were a boy in Minden, ash trees bare in the winter and sheets white as the snow-crowned mountains hanging in the sun, your mother stooped over to gather another piece of laundry out of the basket. She, your father, both of them working from sun-up to sun-down, like you have since age sixteen. No one to appreciate it. Grading road or digging dirt with a backhoe or a clam shell, sweat streaming off your head in the summer, your bones chilled in the winter, and calluses to show for it. Her never appreciating what you brought home. Three years of your life. You told her how a man could love deep as a woman, told her how your father would stand at a distance and admire your mother and she would look back at him after years of marriage and blush because the love in his eyes overwhelmed her. You said that you couldn't settle for less.

You told her everything. Told her how your father killed a man.

You dry the dishes slowly, remembering how early on it was her job, you washing them, her drying, her breast brushing the backside of your arm, and you feeling it all the way to the soles of your feet but especially in your groin. You sip on the Coors for a time, then swallow the last of it, thankful that it didn't make you gag, and you heave the can into the trash. You wonder if it's a trash day and should you take it out. Wonder if you could wrap up the garbage in your head and dump it in a plastic bag.

Before her, you were single and determined to be because nothing you experienced with a woman measured up to what your mom and dad had. You painted Solo Rider in fine cursive aside the tank of your Harley. If you'd had a horse, that would have been your brand. SR for solo rider. Put that to the hindquarter of a fine horse. You look at the Colt resting atop the table. Even in its silence, it's talking. You settled for less, it says. Then adds, you would have forgiven her. If she'd come back. *If.* But she only came back for her clothes. A Reno cop stood in the doorway, hands on his belt close to the handcuffs, glaring at you as if saying, "Do it, boy, so I can hook you up with these." Outside, her new fella leaned back against the seat of her Solstice, reading a newspaper like the events written in small print were more important than what was going on inside your house or inside you, inside your head. And you never laid a hand on her. Ever. Except in love.

You put the dishes away. Everything neat. You grab the broom and sweep, wishing you could turn history into dirt and brush it up in a dust pan and fling it in the wind. This is the broom she once caught you dancing with in the kitchen, Johnny Cash singing "I Walk the Line" on the radio, and she asked what the hell you were doing. And you said, "Waiting for you, my honey," and the two of you danced right there and then you took her into the bedroom and laid her down carefully like she was the brittle page of some mossback book you loved to read. Laid her down on the sheets you burned. Dirt, you think, is a stubborn thing, returns unwanted. Like memories that won't go away. The good ones. The bad ones.

In the bedroom, you open and shut drawers. If you can't find clean clothes, what will this day mean? Seems important. You remember your travel bag in the closet. In it you find two clean pairs of socks and two pairs of underwear. You think of how, as a boy, you wondered why jeans and underwear were called pairs when they were only one. You asked your dad why that was, and he said, "Don't be a dumb one, boy. The damned world's full of dumb ones. Be a little smarter and you'll be way ahead." But your dad never got ahead of anything, except once, and he lost that. His was a sad ending, feeble, mouth hanging open as his jaw ground left to right painfully trying to speak, and not a word half-intelligent coming out, just sounds. You could tell he was saying he was sorry. *Sorry*, a big word and hard to say, especially for him, even when he was all right. The word grew bigger the more he tried to say it and you grew smaller and smaller hearing it. They let you be with him his last day. All you could do was hold his hand and say that it was okay. Okay was a lie.

And that's when you met her. That week when he died. On Virginia Street coming out of Harrah's where she'd been asked to leave because she was taking pictures. She nearly bumped into you, took a step back, saw your Lucchese boots and your straw Stetson and asked where your horse was. You told her you made it a habit not to mount anything with two wheels or four legs. She didn't get it, just stood back and held up her camera, motioned for you to back up a bit, and said, "Smile if you think I'm pretty." You felt her fingers gather around your heart. It was like that. Your dad dying, her coming, and you wide open to it like shutters pulled aside to let the sun in.

YOU TURN ON THE bathroom faucet and look in the mirror. Pretty much the same as yesterday. Jowls bristled. Eyes red. Face crumpled. The water steams up. You spread foam on a week's worth of stubble. Never took to an electric shaver, always seemed a lazy man's way. You spend the next hour grooming yourself, hair combed back, sideburns trimmed. Sunday bright, your mother called it. "Get yourself Sunday bright, son," she'd say. "The gospel's waiting." She was a deep believer, and when she died the whole congregation showed up and maybe every Methodist from Fallon to the North Shore of Lake Tahoe.

You brush your teeth until the enamel shines, just the way you did before going to church. You button your collar, then look at your eyes as you tie the knot on your tie, a Windsor. Your eyes are still red. Nothing can be done about that. You look at the mattress you passed out on the night before and the night before that, and off and on now for days. What was it your mom said? Clean sheets make a bad day go away.

When your dad died, you and four people attended the service. His idea of Sunday was sticking his head under the hood of his '58 Dodge pickup. Your mom said, "Nuts and bolts probably held his brain together and his soul was probably as black as the muffler on that truck." The days she managed to drag him along to church, he would mumble and fidget about in the pew as if he had a bladder full of beer. The day after you married Marie, you told her what your mother had said about your dad, and Marie said she hoped it ran in the family. She was joking. You think of her odd humor as you take a last look in the mirror before switching off the light.

You didn't tell her for the longest time about where your father spent his last years.

⚘ ⚘ ⚘ ⚘ ⚘ ⚘

THE MAN YOU BEAT up, his name is Ansel, Ansel Watson. Who names a boy that? Same parents that didn't teach him to respect other people's marriage vows. You guess that's the case.

You leave the house as if dressed for church. The thing is, it's not Sunday and you have a .357 Magnum tucked in your pant waist and concealed under your coat. It jabs you in the side as you settle in the seat of your pickup. You drive a Ford. An F-150. Your dad hated Fords. Liked Chevies. You wonder if that's why you've always picked them—a little rebellion. Your pickup is eleven years old and paid for. Ansel drives a Nissan Altima with custom chrome wheels. Marie drives a yellow Pontiac Solstice. You make payments on it because the loan is in your name. A full block ahead of you, you saw him drive her car on North Virginia Street near the University, her seated beside him, and you followed him to his house. You didn't have your gun with you or you would have shot him then. Or both of them.

You wonder if your breath smells of beer. The last thing you want is to have a cop snag you for beer breath and red eyes while driving. The convenience store where you usually gas the truck is three blocks away.

The clerk stops what he's doing and stares at your clothes when you lay the packet of gum on the counter. "Going to a wedding or a funeral?" he asks.

"Same difference," you say.

"Sure is. So, what's the occasion?"

You shake your head. "Waterloo."

That puzzles him. He rings up the cost of the gum and asks if that's cash or credit card. You lay down a dollar.

"Ain't enough," he says.

You shrug. "I don't buy gum every day."

On what may be the most important day of your life, you discover gum now costs a hell of a lot more than it did when you were a kid. That kind of day. Gum and you, a going-to-church-dress-up-suit day, and church isn't on the schedule. You pocket the change and leave. As you seat yourself, you realize you just walked into a store with a gun concealed under your coat. You wonder, what's going on in your head, boy? A term your dad used. What if a cop had come in and–? You imagine sirens coming from all directions the way it happened with your dad. You don't want to think about it because you might conjure it. You're no longer walking the line.

Music, you think. Some song to settle jangled nerves. Something to smooth out the ride. The CD case is nearly empty. She got to those too. Left you with one towel and one set of sheets, the ones you burned. Now you flop down on a bare mattress under two blankets. At least you did on nights you didn't pass out on the couch. You wonder how long it had been going on between them. Did she want to get caught? Did she ever love you? You open the CD case. Your choices are four, three Eagles albums and one Johnny Cash. It's not an Eagles day. "Folsom Prison" it is.

You cruise north up Virginia Street in traffic. No hurry. Downtown hasn't changed much. Still downtown. Sometimes you think it's a town on a breathing tank running low on oxygen. You remember going into Harrah's as a kid, your dad's hand resting on your shoulder as you stood in line waiting for the hostess to seat the two of you. Your father said to her, "Just me and my boy here. Boy won himself an award for building a rocket." He squeezed your shoulder. You beamed. She pretended to be impressed. Didn't matter that she wasn't, he was. In those days, you wanted to be a scientist. That was the year he left for Alaska to work on the pipeline, said he had to, that it was the one chance a working man had at making his family comfortable. He came back a different man. Money changed him. He thought he could turn it into a fortune.

You near the University where you attended classes for one semester. Hated it. Others looking at your boots and jeans and straw hat like you were some kind of space alien. That was long after your dad moved the family up from Minden to take work as a welder, after his business constructing stalls went under. He sold the property and the horses and quit team roping. It was the year your mother tripped and cut her head in the fall. She told you in the hospital that she wanted you to have a family. "It's up to you. I'd like a grandchild." But life robbed her of that too.

It seems that cheating is the way of the world. Your dad was cheated out of one hundred seven thousand dollars, the Alaska money. He'd already mortgaged the house to pay her hospital bills, an aging man, his wife dying, left with less than a hundred dollars and his pride. Killed a man over the money, his sentence death by lethal injection in the old gas chamber at the Nevada State Prison. He wished for it instead of life without her. Your dad got cheated and then he tricked the State of Nevada. There's more than one kind of debt. More than one kind of cheating.

You make a turn at the top of the rise. The houses are small, two- and three-bedrooms, built more than sixty years ago, some occupied by student renters. You reach under the seat for the Colt and place it beside you. The song you've been waiting for comes on, prefaced by that thumping guitar rhythm. Patented Johnny Cash, coolest guy in any room.

You turn up the volume and sing.

Not Folsom, you think. Carson City. Where your dad spent his last years. Your pa wasn't humbled even as the cancer bore through his organs. Then the stroke hit, and the diseases sucked his features away until all that remained was a thin sheet of skin over bone and nothing recognizable in his face. He shot a man, as you plan to, then dropped the gun on the dying man's chest and watched him breathe his last. Afterward, he walked out on the lawn where he smoked a cigarette as sirens descended from four directions.

You spot the house on the left, his house, the one you've cruised by for three days now, trying to make up your mind. The white paint on the trim is chipped. The carport's empty. You drive on. She left for a man who lets his house go in need of paint. Probably never had dirty fingernails. The guitar thumps and fades. You pass the house without turning your head. No chrome-wheeled Nissan. You've seen it when you've driven by before. You'll come back. Maybe catch both of them. Him first. Gut shot. Then maybe her. Maybe not. Might be her seeing him bleed to death will be enough, give her a ghost to take to her own grave.

You slip the gun under the seat. Breakfast might help pass the time. Waffles and coffee. You look at the hand that held the gun. It trembles. You wonder if your father's hand trembled before he did it. Calm, the first cop on the scene said, he seemed almost normal. Your pa didn't even take the stand, made no appeal for mercy or asked for clemency. Refused to file writs. But he never saw the gas chamber, never walked up two flights of stairs with his wrists and ankles manacled and into the holding cell to wait out his last hours. The cancer denied the state its demand for justice.

You wonder if you'll do the same.

A few cars and several pickups are parked in the lot. You park beside a Chevy pickup with a shiny toolbox mounted behind the cab. Your dad would like it. The rear window has a decal of a boy pissing on a Ford. You think, *This is the day I could piss on your truck, Mister, and watch you die.*

You take a seat in a window booth. The waitress brings a pot of coffee with her. You order waffles. She asks if you want bacon with them.

"No," you say. The question seems to complicate a morning that's already too complicated.

She pours your cup full. "You look like you need this."

"I do?"

"Look like you've been up all night."

"Yeah."

"Sure you don't want bacon?"

"Sure."

She turns to leave.

"Excuse me," you say.

"Yes."

"Do I look that bad?"

"I'm sorry. I meant, you look tired is all."

You smell bacon and it reminds you of Sunday breakfast with your parents. You wanted what they had, a quiet kind of communal happiness, a slow easy knowing that the smell of bacon and coffee in the morning confirmed. "Changed my mind. I'll have some bacon."

She smiles and nods.

You look around at the customers, all men like you, alone or in pairs. Some bent over a newspaper. Men sipping coffee, conversations held low. *Are their lives full?* you wonder. *Are they happy? Is every life a half-life? People just doing time?*

You eat slowly and have a second and third cup, then pay the bill. You tip the waitress three dollars from the change.

She smiles and says, "Hope you're feeling better now."

Feeling better than what? you think. You nod to her, then go to the men's toilet, urinate and wash your hands. You see your eyes in the mirror. Red's gone, but they don't seem at all clear. You turn your head at an angle and try to recognize the new Bill Brady, but you see a boy of twelve, a kid called Billy, carrying an injured dog half a mile to his home. His eyes had to be different from the ones that look back at you, flat and lost. The eyes of a desperado. A man whose life is frayed.

You don't know this new version of yourself. You know the other you, the man who put in fifty hours a week turning dirt, earning a hard paycheck. You know Billy, the boy who grew up in a decent world, in a family that knew the right thing to do, even if, in the end, your dad didn't take that path. At thirteen, you found an injured mutt left alongside the highway, her front leg broken. Your pa said the vet had to put her down. You pleaded for her, but he insisted it had to be done. When he saw your tears, he said, "Carried her a long way. Maybe you're right." The two of you took the dog home with an amputated leg, named her Lucky and nurtured her. Your dad called her Tripod. She died in your lap nine years later as your pa waited for his date with the executioner. A day that never came.

You remember how he looked when your mom was taken to the hospital the last time. Desperate, lost. He wanted her to live the way you wanted Lucky to. You were nineteen at the time and you couldn't understand his pain. Later, when you visited him in prison to ask why, he said it wasn't just his being cheated. He needed the money to pay for another doctor, another treatment, anything to keep her alive. "When he shrugged," your dad said, "and told me it was my problem, I decided." The papers never printed that. All they wrote was that Avery Brady shot his victim and watched him die. Cold blooded. The jury said first degree with malice.

Malice, a word open to interpretation. A word like *hope* or *love* or *hate* or *jealousy*. The waffles feel as if they have turned to clay in your stomach. You decide you look like a man in pain and turn away from the mirror.

The waitress smiles at you on your way out. "Come again," she says. "Sure."

Inside the truck you reach under the seat and make sure the Colt's still there. It's a small assurance in a world of doubt. Something you need because you don't know yourself. Despite the fact that everything in you screams, "Stay, have another cup and go home," you pull out of the lot like a man on vacation, a man with a life and a half to spare, and drive south toward his house. The three-minute drive takes five minutes. You turn the corner but see no car. The sight of an empty carport cuts into your chest. You switch on the CD player and cruise by. Johnny Cash's baritone breaks the silence. The thump of the guitar matches precisely the pulse at your temple. You just want the ache in your gut to end. Probably the way your father did.

You were happy with her that first year. How did you miss the longing in her eyes? Were you dumb or just hopeful? Leaving for money you might understand, but a man who lives in a house like Ansel's has none. What kind of man is he? What does he offer that you didn't?

As you near the next intersection, you glance in the rearview mirror and see the Altima turn the far corner. You circle the next block and drive up Ansel's street. The Nissan sits in the carport, no one inside it. You drive past and look back through the mirror. You imagine the look on his face when he opens the door, the stark terror in his eyes. Then you picture life fading from them as he lies in his own blood on the floor. You park up the block, take the Colt out and let it rest on your lap, then wait until the song comes on, the words you need to hear.

You shut off the engine, step out, and slam the door. You tuck the Colt into your waistband and slip on your coat, then walk as casually as is possible, given that your knees resist every step. As you near the yard, your hands begin to tremble. A fading blanket of snow covers the ground under the skirt of a blue spruce. Elsewhere the grass is yellow. You notice how the trim on the side of the house was recently painted. You hadn't noticed that before, just the chipped paint in the front. The dormant plants have been cut back. The window shades are up.

You turn left into the driveway. Ten, maybe twelve steps to the front door. No more. As you near the car, the side door to the house opens and a girl of seven or eight runs out. She freezes at the sight of you. The door slams behind her. She isn't supposed to be here. You stare at her, your mouth so dry you can't swallow.

"Daddy," she shouts, "there's a man."

The door opens again and a man roughly your age steps out.

"Can I help you?" he asks.

None of what's happening is a part of the script you wrote in your head, and the man you face off with is not Ansel. You stand there baffled, wondering where the girl came from. And who is this man?

"I said, can I . . ."

The man steps off the stoop and edges his way down the side of the house until he's between you and the girl. The girl grips her father's trousers, her small fingers digging into the cloth. You feel the gun where you've tucked it away.

The father nudges his daughter away. "Go inside," he says to her, then raises his hands and shows you his open palms.

You watch the girl vanish into the house, and you too want to vanish.

"What do you want?" He's confused, but calm, nothing about him exceptional, a man who goes mostly unnoticed in the world. A man like you. Except you're in his driveway with a loaded revolver and wearing a coat and tie and your own confused look.

"The Solstice," you say, seeking some explanation.

"What?"

You point skyward. "Not that kind of solstice. My wife's car. She was in it with you."

"Me?"

"No, I saw Ansel in it. Do you know him?" Your voice cracks. "Is he inside?"

"Never heard of him." He shakes his head. "Are you okay?"

"The Solstice, I saw him driving . . . the yellow Solstice."

"Oh, the yellow Solstice." The man nods and lowers his hands. "I can explain. See, I detail cars. A woman brought hers in, that yellow Pontiac. I shouldn't, but my wife had forgotten something she needed from the house and I . . ."

"Your wife?"

"At work now. She's a receptionist at the hospital. I picked her up in that Solstice and drove her home."

As his words register, you hear ringing in your ears, hear the song drifting away in the back of your head and the thought of killing Ansel that nurtured you for days trails off with that terrible refrain. You and the man stare at one another for a tense moment. Then you notice the girl's confused and worried expression as she looks out the window at the two of you and you realize how you must appear, a man lost, a man out of sorts. This man is not the Bill Brady you would want a young girl to know, not the Bill Brady who wanted a grandchild for his mom.

You look into the man's eyes. "I'm sorry," you say. "It's a mistake."

The man seems less than assured. "You should go. And you don't need that." He points to the bulge where you've concealed the pistol.

The Colt seems even heavier now. Some foreign object. You see your clouded thinking and you hear the heavy thump of the guitar in your head as it fades like a train rumbling off in the distance. Tears begin to trickle down your cheek. You see your breath. Everything inside you stills and you see the day as it is, cold, and the sky sharp and clear as any you have ever seen. You think of the nights that came to own you, nights spent twisting your guts in knots, nights you sat in the dark clicking the cylinder, dumping bullets on the mattress where the two of you made love, and then feeding them back into the cylinder, the malice growing inside you. You imagine your father dropping a gun on a dead man's chest, then picture your mother hanging sheets, her fingers numb from the cold and your father coming out with a cup of coffee that he hands her. You see your dad reach into the basket of laundry and finish her work. That kind of love. A working man's love, the kind of love present in the man before you.

"I didn't mean to upset your daughter. Or you."

"I'm going inside now," he says and backpedals a step.

"You detail cars?"

He nods, takes another step, then stops and stares at you. "You don't look so good. Is there someone? Do you have a car?"

"My wife left me," you say. "Another man." You say it to someone for the first time, to a stranger who doesn't need your mess in his life, and you hear the plaintive words of a hundred songs, the lyrics of heartbreak—this time yours.

"That's—I've got to go see to my daughter. You scared her. I mean—"

His voice trails off and a wall of silence sits between you and him. His eyes are locked onto yours and you recognize in his something that's been lost in yours for too long. "I don't know what," he says breaking the silence, "to say, but whatever you have in mind, you shouldn't do it."

"I'm sorry. It was a bad mistake," you say, but you mean more than what the words say. You turn away from him and walk numbly to the street, wiping at your eyes with the back of your hand.

"I won't tell anyone," he calls to you. You look back over your shoulder and nod. "It's okay," he hollers. "We'll forget this."

You grip the cold door handle of your truck and pause to look back. The man still looks in your direction. You clear the Colt's cylinder and set the gun aside on the seat, then raise your hand and wave to him. You settle in the seat and as you do you notice the mountains where the Truckee flows. You recall fishing the river at dawn with your father, his thick fingers tying a leader, water foaming against the banks, the spring sun slanting through the tall ponderosa. The snowpack will melt soon and begin restoring the cycle of life, a trickle here, a trickle there, the same way you'll be putting yours back in order. Sheets, you think, you'll be needing new sheets. Those first. No one should sleep for long on a bare mattress. Then you turn the ignition key, knowing now that it's over. You can claim the rest of your days.

the road to mandalay without laughter

A breeze flowed in, carrying the smell of the harbor, exhaust fumes from traffic below, and her perfume. He remembered the smell of her perfume, as he remembered the earthy, intimate scent of her when they'd made love. A half mile away, the bay shimmered black and silver, and the lethargic summer sun dipped toward the western horizon. *The same routine for a few billion years*, Connor thought, *wouldn't that wear after a while? Wouldn't that be dull?* Beside him on the patio table sat a nearly empty bottle of zinfandel. He poured the last of the wine into his glass and gazed at Barbara. She looked away.

He could easily thump out this scene on a keyboard—the protagonist brushing off the crumbs of a past life, a younger woman, the moment sparking with tension, unresolved matters that eventually move toward resolution, if not redemption. Their circumstances were the premise of ten thousand fictions. Even as he looked at her, he began to compose it as a story in his head. But this wasn't at all like brushing off stale crumbs. And it wasn't fiction. And he saw no good resolution.

She was thirty-nine now, and he fifty-one, too old for the scene he'd write. Ten years before they'd been lovers. Their potential had seemed more, but the outcome had been less, for him much less. He'd struggled for five years before landing a tenure-track job at a small college, and another three passed before he signed his first book contract. She'd dumped him for a man with money, not boundless wealth but enough to provide comfort and some luxury, and dropped out of graduate school.

She'd been silent for some time. How long, he couldn't be sure. He was feeling the wine and remembering what he'd tried to forget— how it had been with them, the spontaneous and impulsive behavior. He wondered how far he could push matters. Could he reach across the table and take her hand? He felt certain she would welcome it. And he could flatter her as he once had. Not with the same conviction, not with the ardor that had once pressed relentlessly against his chest like a car jack. Not anything like that.

As she gazed off where the sun hung above the bay, he studied her profile. She was striking, her face angular, her cheekbones pronounced, forehead high and unwrinkled. But it was her hands he always noticed, hands he once held, hands that touched his body with an intimacy that made him shiver. Even as a graduate student she was always elegantly restrained in her choice of clothing, never anything gaudy. Now she wore a navy-blue and gold Versace silk dress, and as always, no make-up. Here she was at a table with him in a perfect setting for a reunion of lovers. For years he'd envisioned variations of this approximate scenario–Barbara across from him, a colored evening sky, a breeze, wine, conversation marked by sexual undercurrents. There was a preface to the encounter: he was to be published, and Barbara was to attend a reading or some such event in Phoenix where he would look out and see her in the audience; his eyes would isolate her from the crowd, and for a moment it would appear he was reading just to her.

What he'd fantasized taking place one way in Phoenix actually took place abruptly and unexpectedly as he was autographing books at Granville & Taylor Fine Books in San Diego and he'd been unprepared for it. She'd materialized in the aisle, thrust an open book toward him, and said, "Make it to Barbara, with fond regards." He'd said he couldn't write anything so lame, signed it, thanked her without looking up, and said goodbye. She'd waited outside the book store, and now here they were.

He'd been angry at her for years, and perhaps the anger may have gone on unchecked, but much of it dissolved the day she'd called to tell him Angie had killed herself. With a shotgun at age thirty-four. It was news that changed the past the way an earthquake alters the landscape.

Angie, Connor thought, *you had the best chance among us.* He simply couldn't picture her dead. There had been too much life to her. He remembered the three of them taking turns on a trampoline, Angie propelling herself upward and hanging there, legs apart, fingers grasping the tips of her toes, then tucking and falling gracefully, Barbara, fearful and as clumsy as she often accused herself of being. But for an instant she'd defied gravity and had seemed ethereal, her waist-length hair suspended beside her head like wings holding her in the air. He'd fallen in love at that very moment. He wondered if it was a dream he'd created. Now, this chance encounter with the woman who'd so deeply wounded him seemed merely a curiosity, perhaps a chance to feed his damaged ego. After all, he had his book now, and the pain had been subsumed by the darkness left from Angie's death.

Nearby, a couple entwined hands and stared at one another. They were his age, and when he thought about their apparent happiness, Connor felt a loss. Where's the intrigue? After a certain age, don't we just follow a template, merely go through the motions? *Why*, he wondered, *is seeing young lovers so much more–?* He didn't like the words that came to mind, especially *palatable*.

He could tell Barbara how much it pained him to call up old memories, follow up that with an invitation to go dancing. He could try to seduce her. She was unhappy. Obvious signs. Not mentioning the husband, etc.

"May I make a toast?" he asked. *Angie, Angie*, he thought as he lifted his glass.

Barbara had barely touched her wine. "Is this your way of getting me to drink? You know I can't handle wine. And then what? You'd be stuck with a drunk woman."

He held his glass up and waited. She hesitated then touched hers to his.

"Remember, I'm a married woman," she said, as if it were both humorous and serious.

He nodded–at last, the husband. She had to bring that to the forefront. "To the Road to Mandalay," he said.

"What?"

He grinned. "Yes."

"God, I'd forgotten." She looked over her glass at him as she touched the rim to her lips.

How could she forget it? The Road to Mandalay was their story, the three of them. He took a swallow and set his glass down. "So, we meet in San Diego. Who'd have thought it?"

"I happened on your picture in the paper. I was amazed."

"That I published a book?" He knew her well enough to realize this was no coincidence. She'd come intentionally, but to admit as much might compromise her. She'd often used white lies for effect, to distance herself from her own truths. She likely believed some of them, might even believe this one. "Surprise, surprise," he said.

"Don't be like that," she said.

He thought of how badly he'd missed her. In that painful and unwanted separation, he'd hoped that she'd call and ask him to come get her. She called, but she didn't ask him to come– discouraged him, in fact. After his departure to find work, she'd detached herself from him almost immediately and eventually drifted into the life of a man who picked her out of a crowd in a bar. Even now, he had difficulty believing she'd thrown aside the promise of that day in Jerome, them laughing as she plucked a blossom from a honeysuckle bush. They'd held hands and looked out over the Verde Valley, and that moment in its honesty had seemed close to something wondrous.

"What were you thinking just then?" Barbara asked.

He blinked, and when he looked at her this time, she seemed older than her thirty-nine years. "I was thinking about the drive we took to Las Vegas, how we stopped in Jerome and you plucked honeysuckle off a bush for me to taste."

She took a sip and set the wine in front of her. "I was thinking how nice it is that Connor Haynes finally got his book, but it came so late."

"Too late for you."

She tilted her head and raised an eyebrow, but didn't address the obvious challenge.

Silence and lies. Back to games, Connor thought. "So how is paradise?"

She shook her head. "It's not a perfect marriage. None are."

Just then the waiter came to gather plates and pour coffee. He was efficient and almost noiseless, no intrusive questions, a simple, "May I bring something else?"

Connor ordered a snifter of Benedictine, and when the waiter was out of earshot, he asked if her husband brought her to this restaurant when they visit her in-laws?

Barbara laid her napkin on her lap, and patted it. "How'd you know about the in-laws?"

"Angie was my friend too."

She was silent for a brief moment, as if shuffling through his statement to find the other layers, then asked, "How's the book doing?"

"It's enough to get tenure, but no one gets rich on books like that."

"You must be pleased."

"About job security?"

"That's cynical, even for you," she said.

He smiled. He wanted to pursue what he knew she wanted to avoid. "Hell, I could own a dry-cleaners and make a lot more."

"Don't," she said.

"Oh, I have nothing against dry-cleaning. It contributes. Cleanliness and godliness, don't they go hand in hand?"

"Stop it, please."

"Sure."

She smiled. "I kept everything you ever wrote back then."

"I suppose that's something."

"Jesus, let up. You make dry-cleaning sound dirty."

He held a smile waiting for her to realize what she'd said. Finally, she smiled. For a period, they were quiet.

"I apologize," he said, breaking the silence. He knew he could be ugly and didn't want to misbehave, not this badly. He raised an eyebrow and grinned. "But you did dump me, or dump on me. Pick the expression."

He remembered a night they'd thrown away the sheets left over from her first marriage, a symbol of sorts. After making love, they'd lain on the bare mattress, talking vaguely of love without ever saying the words until sleep saved them from saying too much.

"Not exactly." She stared at him flatly. "You left."

Connor figured she would sanitize the truth. He'd left to find work, had intended to come back for her after she finished her degree. He nodded, remembering how impotent he'd felt, loving her as he had, knowing it was not enough. "And ended up competing with dry-cleaning. Really, how could I win?"

Connor looked over at the middle-aged couple. They were no longer holding hands, but were leaned into each other in intimate conversation. *Perhaps*, he thought, *we can make new templates.* How long had it been since he felt anything strong stir inside him for anything other than writing? She had pushed him deep inside himself, and there was a backlog of words on pages, hundreds of pages waiting now, because of her, her and Angie.

"Do you work with him?" It seemed a fair question.

She lowered her eyes. "I helped until I had the miscarriage."

"I didn't know."

"Actually three." She clasped her hands and rubbed them together. Her face darkened. The pitch in her voice had shifted. "The last one, you could see its little hands. They were like doll's hands. It was a boy." She picked up the wine and tossed the rest of it down.

He resisted an impulse to take her hand. "I'm sorry," he said. Guilt. What a strange beast. She felt none for what she'd done intentionally, but he could sense that these miscarriages, which were out of her control, made her ashamed.

Connor downed the last of his wine, then asked what seemed both the obvious question and obvious answer. "Why don't you adopt?"

She shook her head. "You never know with adoption what you'll get."

"Actually, you kind of do know."

"Well, that's my husband's thinking. Besides, there is another way."

She explained the complexities that accompany *in vitro* fertilization, the expense, how she needed donor eggs because hers were irregularly formed. She'd found a surrogate to carry the child. To him, she sounded like someone outlining a business strategy based on probabilities and outcomes, and as she explained, seemed to be justifying herself to herself. Connor listened closely, trying not to be judgmental, but ultimately the procedure sounded too synthetic, too designed. *A designer child*, he thought. Children should come, it seemed to him, from possibility, from chance. But he reconsidered. *Who am I to judge?*

The waiter brought coffee and a snifter. He set the Benedictine in front of Connor and quietly left. As he listened to Barbara, Connor sipped on the liqueur and glanced over her shoulder at the couple. The man pulled the woman's chair out. It seemed exaggerated and awkward on his part, but the woman accepted the gesture graciously. They seemed happy and unconcerned. She folded her arm into his, and they walked off. Now, arms entwined and moving, they took on a different aspect, graceful even. Connor thought how he and Barbara had been—anxious kisses, the two of them yielding to the moment, like the time they were driving east on the Carefree Highway and she'd stripped and told him to pull over.

When he looked back, Barbara was staring at her cup.

"Now it's a matter of waiting," she said.

"Waiting. Yes." He understood waiting.

Barbara said, "What's ironic is that Angie was pregnant. Her husband wanted her to have an abortion. She'd had an abortion, you know, when she was young. Just as I did."

The cup rattled as she set it in the saucer. "I still think about it. It's unfair. She wanted that baby but killed herself and it."

Connor swallowed the Benedictine and looked at the cleft in the skyline where earlier the bay had been shimmering. The sun had spilt over the horizon and bled into the water. The ocean was red and gulls circled overhead.

"She told me all about you, Barbara," he said.

"Told you about what?"

"It's in the past, but I wanted you to know." There was something about her deliberate planning of the baby that made him want to be cruel, but he was also ashamed of himself. He could write these little psycho-fictive dramas but was no good at living one. He should call for the check, pay it, and tell her it was a mistake to meet like this, his fault, but that seemed too dramatic.

"I deserve this, I guess," she said.

He shrugged. "She was my friend too. Take it as that."

"Yeah. Why didn't you come to the service?"

The reason was her being there, her and her husband, and what others might think. He shrugged, which seemed answer enough. They stared at one another a moment, then she broke the eye contact and lifted her cup. As she sipped her coffee, he looked where the other couple last sat, the table now cleaned off, and he thought of an afternoon when the three of them had gone to car lots to drive four-wheel-drive vehicles they couldn't afford but pretended they could. He played the buyer, taking the role of a stockbroker or an attorney. Barbara admired his panache; Angie just laughed. Afterward they shared pizza and talked about literature and a dreamy future when all the education and hardship would be behind them. But they talked without commitment, for that would shatter the illusion.

Barbara lowered her cup. "What did she tell you?"

"She told me to stop moping, to put you behind me. She was concerned I'd stop writing. She told me about Dave and about the musician you were sleeping with when I wasn't around, and . . . Should I go on?"

She looked over her tilted cup. She didn't dispute anything, just said, "You left me."

He remembered how she'd sat back on the couch and looked at him and had said that he was over forty, that he had no position. She had reduced his humanity to this simple equation. He nodded. "You wouldn't commit. There were no jobs. I was over forty."

"Maybe there's more to it."

"Maybe. But those were your words."

They were silent for some time after that exchange. Barbara reached across the table and squeezed his hand. She said she had hoped he'd come to the service for Angie, that she'd looked for him and was disappointed. The three of them had been close, hadn't they?

He recalled the night spring semester ended and they'd sat on the floor, the three of them, on pillows to watch an old-movie channel and stuffed themselves on chips and brownies until dawn. *The Road to Zanzibar* was the last movie to play. They'd laughed at the antics no matter how silly or predictable, laughed until the pressures of the semester faded and their bellies hurt and their faces were red, until their eyelids drooped and it was time to sleep. He and Barbara went to their bed. A few minutes later they heard Angie vomiting. Barbara tried to stop him, but he shook her off and went to the bathroom. Angie was crying. He'd cleaned her up, helped her into a fresh pajama top, wiped her mouth with a damp towel, then flushed the bowl and carried her to their bedroom. She'd cried until all of them were again laughing, this time at the sadness of everything. She'd slept with them most of the day, gathered up in their arms like an oversized foundling.

"What about Angie? What do you think?"

"You mean what do I feel?"

When they'd met, Angie was just another student writer trying to get her stories to float and living, as he had, from rejection to rejection without money in the bank. Then she found a tenured job with a community college, married, and soon all had gone awry. Suicide. In a statement to the police the husband had claimed she'd said there would be nothing to come back to. She'd been nothing if not impulsive.

The waiter came by and lit the gas lights. He smiled at them as one smiles at lovers. Connor wanted to tell him how wrong he was. He looked at the flame in the gas light. "A lot of women pick the wrong men, but they don't kill themselves. How do I feel?"

"She was over the weekend before. She seemed normal. She talked about the future. It didn't make sense."

"You've forgotten how she was."

There were nights they'd hear her in the bathroom retching. It was painful to listen to, even the flushing of the bowl. And the careless way Angie played poker, raising the pot to more than any of them could afford, and her trying to fill an inside straight. Had Barbara forgotten the truck Angie bought? Weren't the test rides supposed to be a gag? She'd put herself in debt to live on the edge. Worst of all were the men. She was ransacked by every jerk she brought home.

"We were all a bit messy, but she couldn't sit and eat a good meal, couldn't taste pepper or garlic," he said. "What kind of life is it if you can't enjoy food?"

Barbara rubbed her eyes with the backs of her hands. She looked at him, her eyes searching, "I want you to know I took precautions. My last pregnancy I stayed in bed for almost five months, took every precaution. I miscarried in the bed. There was blood everywhere. He came in and asked what to do. What to do? I told him he had to drive me to the hospital. He said, 'What about the baby?'"

Connor nodded. He told her that he was confident she'd done everything, that he knew she didn't take chances. He knew this from how she parceled out her affection. He recalled the last visit, him walking behind her across campus and her picking up the pace, so as to avoid being noticed with him. She never took chances, not those kinds.

The waiter returned and asked if they cared for more coffee. Barbara said yes. Connor asked for the bill. When the waiter was gone, Connor leaned back and studied her face, still peculiarly enchanting, especially in the dim light. "Remember our first lunch, the one you missed?"

"Should I?"

"I folded up a piece of white paper and made . . . No, you shouldn't."

"I remember. You made a snowflake, and I was flattered until you explained the flake was a metaphor for me. It was cruel."

Connor smiled. "Angie thought it was funny."

As the waiter poured her coffee, Barbara watched the cup fill and Connor looked past her at the ocean. Connor seemed to float away into the past, the three of them in front of the television practicing two slaps on the knee, three claps of the hand, three patty cakes, then turn and swing with a right cross and knock the bums out. Beat up the bad guys and get a laugh.

Angie had come up with the idea to go on the Road to Mandalay. She and Barbara dressed in his short-sleeve shirts and chinos and wrapped him in a sarong improvised from an old sheet. They painted his face with makeup, cheeks and lips bright red, eyes darkened with mascara, and pinned oval earrings on his ears, then wrapped an orange towel on his head. They claimed that he was prettier than Dorothy Lamour. The three of them walked the sidewalk pretending to be in a rain forest in Mandalay . . . two slaps on the knees, three claps of hands, three–

"What did you do when you first heard about Angie?" he asked.

"Do?"

"What did you do?"

"I was shocked. Mad. I thought her husband killed her."

"But what did you do?"

"I called the police to tell them I suspected the husband."

He wanted to hear that she'd cried for her as he had. "Ah."

He looked at her face, the face that had once brought him joy. It was a lovely face, even now. He thought about the un-legislated crimes people commit, self-killing to kill the pain of loss, the killing of love itself, the remorseless betrayal of trust, and the self-made prison people exile themselves to rather than risk heartbreak. He recalled the dark days of his own emptiness, days that kept him handcuffed to the keyboard for a decade looking for purpose as words marched across a page and each page moved toward being a book.

We are all criminals, he thought, *and victims. We live much of life in that space between things, between fantasy and reality, hope and despair, creation and destruction, love and loss. We are sleepers in a world that begs us to be awake. We too are like Angie, chasing image and illusion, looking for a road to Mandalay filled with carefree laughter. We forget the nights of her isolation in a bathroom gagging out meals. We plant life wherever we can, in petri dishes or, artificially, in words.*

The bay had turned a shimmering black. *If Angie were here alive*, he thought, *we would walk through the brightly lit mezzanine shops remarking on what we would buy when our books made us famous.* It was always fame, not riches. Riches were out of reach. He'd lay an arm over her shoulder and they'd laugh. Pretense seemed much more satisfying. He stared at the ocean. In his despair, Angie provided the words he needed: "She's not worth it, write." He'd heard only the part about writing. He'd hung on to memories of Barbara, adding to them until they were as cumbersome as pockets filled with stones. Why hadn't Angie taken her own advice?

"What are you looking at?" Barbara asked and looked over her shoulder.

He said, "It's dark. I have to be going." He wished it had gone better. In what way, he wasn't sure.

"I have to drive back to Phoenix in the morning. Will you wait until I finish my coffee?"

"Sure."

She drank slowly, seemingly in thought. After he paid the check, she asked if he'd walk her to her car. It was dusk by then and so shadowed the unlit buildings seemed indistinct, and he and she were part of the shadows. He said he hoped her marriage and businesses went well. It was time for that kind of conversation and the inhibitions that accompany it. Between sentences they walked to the sounds of their own footsteps on the concrete and the occasional passing car. When they reached her Saab, she offered him a ride to his hotel. He shook his head.

"Why'd you want to know what I did when I heard the news?" she asked.

What he really wanted to know was if she could feel sadness. If she cradled enough love inside to feel a deep sense of needless loss. Her windows were rolled down so they could talk. He told her it wasn't important. She seemed puzzled and again offered a ride.

"Thanks, but I think I'll walk. The weather's great for a walk."

She nodded, but made no immediate effort to start the car. "I guess this is goodbye."

"Yes. Goodbye."

"I drove here to see you," she confessed. "My marriage is . . . I just don't know."

"I figured as much. But I hope it works out, the baby and all." As he said it, he knew he meant it, and it made him feel lighter.

She started the engine. Like her clothing, the car was expensive, tasteful, and very safe, like the life she'd chosen. He pictured Angie on the trampoline again, reckless and graceful, high above them smiling, then closing her eyes as she tucked into a ball and descended. That was what was gone, recklessness and grace. And that as much as anything was what he'd mourned when Barbara had called to tell him about the suicide.

He looked at Barbara's eyes, large and brown, and the eyelids that he'd once kissed. Her eyes were a big part of the fiction that he'd created about her, about them, one that had been hard to put aside. Earlier in the evening the truth had seemed too minuscule to matter, but was it important here because it seemed like a gate? He cleared his throat. "I didn't attend because I didn't want to be in a room with you and others who knew us and would be aware of the two of us. Didn't want those connections made. I was just too small and selfish."

The thought lingered a moment, but she didn't pursue it. She said, "Will I like the book?"

"You'll like the next one." It sounded like a promise. He leaned in the passenger side window. "I wanted to know, did you cry when you heard about her?"

"What kind of question is that?" she asked.

He stood away from the window. "No kind. No kind of question at all. I hope it goes well with your pregnancy."

"Yes."

She pulled away.

It was two blocks to his hotel. He wondered what her future would be, then decided hers would be a continuum of the present, no surprises. His immediate future was the five-hour drive to Las Vegas in the morning. There would be plenty of time to play events out in his head. He saw no reason to hurry through the calm space of night, and he let the cool embrace of the ocean breeze carry him along. The next moment, he was taken by an odd urge. He stopped and looked about. Bending his knees, he leaned forward, slapped his thighs twice, clapped three times, patty-caked, then spun about and threw an awkward punch at the vacant air, thinking, *We were silly. We were alive.*

double irish

When we settled here, I didn't know about Kingman's population of meth heads, didn't know about the dregs in Golden Valley, didn't know Timothy McVey and that Terry clown had set up their terrorist business on the outskirts of Kingman. When I came upon the town, I was merely looking for a place to raise my son and daughter free of what I'd seen as a kid. No gangs, no violence, safe schools, no smog. Those seemed more important than making sixty grand a year or more in San Bernardino. I'd scouted out opportunities to start a business in Tucson, Flagstaff, and Prescott. My top choice was Prescott and I was on my way to check out a house there when I stopped for lunch at the Hot Rod Café on Hualapai Mountain Road.

I had a two-hour ride ahead, so I took a seat on the patio and relaxed from the ride with a cup of coffee. Looking around at the mountains and clean air, I thought, *What the hell. This isn't so bad.* When the waiter came out to refresh my coffee, I asked what brought him here.

"The Witness Protection Program," he said, offering up a wry smile that left me to determine if he was telling the truth or not.

True or not, I thought in an odd turn, *if federal cops figure it's safe enough for a witness, why not for my family?* I drove around and checked out the cost of houses. Three hours later I found a four-bedroom ranch house on an acre that I could pay cash for once I sold the house in San Berdoo. I put up a grand in earnest money and drove home. At first Maura didn't like the idea, but she came around when she walked into the house of her dreams at half the price of the cramped developer box we'd bought in California.

That was nine years ago.

We've been happy here, still are. Some hard ripples in the marriage, like all couples have. Some difficulties that come with parenting teenagers. We manage. Her, me, our kids Ronnie and Beth, we have our disputes, but there's a lot of love in our house. At night before the lights go out, we mend our differences by mentioning in some way that we care for one another. Words count just as much as actions.

Anyhow, when we first settled into the new life, Kingman was in the midst of a growth cycle, a boom in fact, almost like the eighties heyday in Southern Cal. Two golf courses and generally good weather attracted a population of retired types. Developers leveled ground and slapped up middle-class homes as fast as a contestant on *Jeopardy* can press a thumb buzzer. Investors bought up houses almost that fast. One month a vacant lot, the next a stucco house with a tile roof and a covered patio. Mostly nice people moved here, though their driving habits sometimes sparked my nerves. I enjoyed my work, especially the times I made people a little safer by securing their doors or came to the rescue when one was locked out of a home or car.

Like the construction business, mine boomed. I hired two workers. Trained them both myself and bonded them. A locksmith must be bonded. It's a matter of public trust. I like to ask people, who do they trust more, a locksmith or a politician? Ella, the first employee I hired, was in her mid-forties and a quick learner. Lenny was much younger and a bit slow, but determined. I enjoyed teaching them. Passing on knowledge makes you feel good. They worked hard, and the demand for our service kept us all making a good living. At the end of the workday, we'd sit in the office and trade stories, kind of like a family. The house, the work, the kids doing well, it was the American Dream, not one everybody would appreciate, but one I did.

I kind of believe in karma and bad history, like the supposed patriots blowing up a federal courthouse makes bad karma. It was in the air, but for five years I did well despite that lurking bad karma. Then when it came, it landed hard, thanks to big banking, people's greed, and poor government oversight. Then the economy dumped. Construction stopped. Billfolds squeaked when someone opened one and pulled out a dollar.

For the Kingman area, it was like lighting a match to a gasoline-soaked sheet of tissue paper, and the little guy was the one who got burned. My business was no different from others connected to construction. I had to let Lenny go. Kept Ella on the payroll for a year before I gave her the bad news. It wasn't easy in either case, but I had a family and the business was all I had to pay the mortgage and put groceries in the refrigerator. Ella waits tables up at the resort in the Hualapais now. Lenny, he moved on. Don't know where.

Maura, my redheaded love, keeps the books and handles the calls when I'm not in. She does it from home so we can keep our lives separated a little. Always thinking about our being happy. Now I make the overhead in a different way. Houses go empty. For Sale signs go up. Locks need to be switched out. Most of my income comes from re-keying locks on repossessed or abandoned houses, and I work for a handful of mortgage companies, two local banks and three real estate agencies. They don't want the locks replaced, just rekey the old ones. I have no idea who lived in the houses or the circumstances that led to their loss. I don't meet people the way I used to. That was a bonus to the job, hearing other people's stories. Like the waiter who said he was here because of the Witness Protection Program.

It's amazing what people will do, what they have done, to a place when a bank hits them with a foreclosure. I see it all the time. Houses gutted of appliances, electrical fixtures, faucets and even toilets. Just a hole left in a bathroom floor. It's sad. My business doesn't require me knowing what their circumstances were. I ignore the damage and blight, do the job, change the tumbler sequences and write up an invoice.

Then there are the ones you can't ignore.

Three weeks ago, I got a call to an isolated address in Golden Valley, a manufactured house on several acres, a place where a person might grow melons or keep horses. The valley lies to the north of Kingman in a desert basin, a sprawl of manufactured houses, trailers and metallic garages that look like miniature airplane hangars. I don't mean to judge, but calling it Golden seems a bit like calling a block of coal a diamond. That stretch of desert's probably home to more misfits per capita than Skid Row in L.A. You don't drive there unless it's for business or you're headed to Laughlin to graze a buffet with the family and watch the Colorado flow by.

I parked my pickup in front of a faded-gray double-wide with its roof nearly collapsed at one corner. I'd seen a lot of houses in disrepair. This one was nearly demolished. The real estate salesman Jimmy Bowler was in his car talking on his cell phone. I stepped out of my truck and walked over and stood beside his car.

Spread like brass seeds over the yard were expended casings of

.22s, 30-06s, .38s and 9mms. The only time I'd seen that much brass before was at a firing range. The front of the house bore signs of the shooter's proclivities, a shattered porch light, three bullet holes in a faux weather vane, a satellite dish on the roof with so many bullet holes it looked like a colander.

Jimmy stepped out of his car and stood beside me. "Can't wait to see what's inside."

I thought, *Well, I can.*

I went to work on the door. Four locks on the front doors, two each on the security door, same on the inner door, no lock set alike. I couldn't pick them and it took twenty-five minutes to drill them. Then I discovered that the front door was double barred. A door must be barred from the inside, so I knew whoever barred it had to come out of a door that wasn't. I drilled the side door to the garage, then the inside door that led to the interior of the house.

Roaches scurried about under a layer of newspapers spread out wall to wall. Jimmy breezed by and went into the kitchen and shortly called to me in a fractured voice. Where an electrical fixture above the sink had once been, a cord tied in a hangman's noose hung down. A rubber baby doll, the kind my daughter used to play with, dangled at the end of the cord, a steak knife plunged in its chest. A note pinned to its diaper read, "Death's Child."

Something about that doll struck me. It seemed an assault on little girls, my own daughter. I would've, from that point, rekeyed the locks and left, but Jimmy had to assess the damage to the place, so I followed him from room to room. I didn't want him to feel alone. The place was trashed throughout, nothing new. What made it exceptional was that hung on the walls in every room were posters of celebrities, all of them riddled with bullet holes. On the ceiling in the master bedroom someone had spray painted a large black swastika and the number eighty-eight. A mouse squirmed around under a pile of magazines and newspapers in one corner.

Jimmy said, "I can't sell it. The bank'll eat this one. Let's get done and get gone."

If a place ever needed an exorcism, that place did. I left there feeling grim and thinking that perhaps things I took for granted in my life, even my family's life, were an illusion I'd fabricated, that everything that held matters together was vulnerable. I don't usually take my work home. I want to be strong for them, but that night Maura knew something was bothering me. She asked if it was something a shot of Irish could help. She meant it two ways, her being Irish and my taste for a well-aged single-malt. I told her I'd probably need both to forget what I saw. After a drink on the patio, I loosened up and described the scene. She listened. We're good that way, always taking time to listen. When I finished describing what I'd seen, she said, "I feel dirty all over." I knew there'd be no double Irish that night. She took a long bath and spent the night staring at the ceiling until she drifted off. Me, I stayed awake much longer.

I might have put that experience behind me, but four days ago I got a call to go to an address in Valle Vista, a stable, well-kept residential area off Route 66. The houses sit on quarter- and half-acre lots and are mostly stick and stucco, nice places built for nice people. Gale, a rep from a mortgage company, was waiting at the front. She waved as I drove up. I grabbed my tool bag and slammed the truck door.

"This one'll be easy. I just need keys to turn over to a realtor."

I told her I could use easy because I had two calls backed up and needed some lunch.

It was a simple two-lock system. I picked the lock and we were in. The inside was immaculate, floors swept and mopped, carpet recently cleaned, walls freshly painted, the cabinets and light fixtures all in good order. Hardly what I was used to seeing in a repo. We both commented on the good condition of the house. "An easy sell," Gale said and noted something on a form on her clipboard.

All I had to do was rekey the front and the back and the side door to the garage, and I was on my way. Easy. I went to the back door and started to work. It's a breeze taking off the knobs and taking the hardware to the truck to reset the tumblers. I had the first one off in three minutes and was about to do the same with the guts on the side door lock when Gale called out from a backroom, "Oh, my God."

Unsure what might have startled her, I dropped my bag and the hardware on the kitchen counter and hurried to the master bedroom. She stood in the threshold to the bath, her clipboard hanging at her side in one hand, her other hand covering her mouth.

"What's the matter?" I asked.

She answered by pointing inside. I stepped through the threshold. It was a large bathroom, a faux marble two-sinker with a ten-foot mirror. Taped on the mirror were more than two dozen photographs of people at different stages of life and written beneath the photos in lipstick were their names, date and place of birth, and the year and location of when and where the photos were taken. On the counter top, five sheets of neatly arranged pages lay torn from a legal pad, the words stroked in with a practiced cursive, the handwriting of a woman who treats writing as an art form. Beside the last sheet of paper was a black book that read *Journal.*

Behind me, Gale sank to the floor and sat there trying not to cry. She'd been working repos for a long while and was hardened to the task. This reaction was unlike her or any of the women in her profession I'd met. I asked if she'd be okay.

"Yeah, but not right away. Ben from the legal department told me that after she got a foreclosure notice, the owner drove herself to Flagstaff and tried suicide. Someone found her. Pills, he said. I think she's with her daughter."

I went to the countertop and noted that the sheets of paper were numbered one through six, the first titled, "Myself," the second through the fifth, "My Family." I read enough from the second sheet to know that the writer was named Katie Lowe and she was seventy-two. She wrote that her husband of forty-nine years had died two years before. The next sheet said her father, pictured as number one, had been a soldier and participated in the Normandy Invasion. I looked at the faded black-and-white snapshot, its edges yellowing. The man depicted was tall and thin, his mid-twenties, dressed in an Ike jacket, above his pocket the emblems of his service. His hand rested on the shoulder of a blonde girl about five years old. He was smiling for the picture. The little girl looked confused. Below the picture Katie Lowe had written, "Albert D. Lowe, my father and me, March, 1946."

I looked at Gale. "Did you read any of this?"

"Some." She shook her head. "I'll have all of it cleaned out. And returned to her."

What would compel someone who was losing a house to the mortgage company to clean so thoroughly only to leave this family history behind?

Gale seemed to read my thoughts. "It's sad," she said.

I gazed for a time at the yellow sheets of papers. An old woman, left alone in a house she could no longer afford, sat somewhere in the same house with a notepad on her lap and recorded her history for strangers to find, words that said someone lived. No, words that said someone lived *here*. I didn't read any further, couldn't. I imagined Maura under other circumstances sitting and writing our history in the house she loved. Then I thought of the countless houses I'd rekeyed in recent years and the untold histories left among the silent walls of vacant rooms.

I helped Gale to her feet and went about my job. But I kept being distracted by the idea of photos and images of my own family replacing those on the mirror. While ruminating on what I'd seen, I did something that astonished me even as I did it. I made an extra key for the house, something I'd never done before, an act that under other circumstance would seem unethical to me. I handed the keys, all but that one, to Gale before I drove away.

I waited in my pickup beside the convenience store on Route 66 and watched for Gale to pass by, after which I drove back to the house and let myself in. I knew that what I was doing was strange and some might think illegal, but I felt an obligation. As I turned the key in the lock, my pulse beat heavily at my temples. I heard the chatter of a lawn mower on the golf course two hundred yards away. Inside, I smelled the lingering odors, Gale's perfume, a faint pine scent, and scrubbing soap.

I went to the bathroom and thumbed through the tablet. The third page was spotted with coffee stains that she'd wiped away. She'd written over the smudged words. I took down the family photos one at a time to gain an idea of who was who. After replacing each in its right spot, I took the journal to the bedroom and opened the drapes. I sat in a corner and began reading page after page, every word written in the same careful looping cursive.

I read about her daughter, a divorced mother of a teenager, and Katie's son who contracted AIDS and died at age forty in a bedroom in her house, perhaps the one I was sitting in. She wrote proudly of her granddaughter whose ambition at age nine was to find a cure for cancer. The last pages charted her husband's desperate struggle with his disease. A career fireman, he'd retired as an assistant chief. She'd spent their life savings and mortgaged the house in order to take him to Europe for experimental treatments to save him, but to no avail.

She closed with, "I have no regrets except that I couldn't meet my obligations. My husband and I were happy, I more so because I gave my all to those dearest to me. I've always met my obligations and took pride in that fact, but now I'm ashamed."

I set the journal aside, then I walked the empty rooms, my mind struggling to reconcile the sadness I was witnessing and not just hers. I thought about her alone in a house emptied of the love of family and then about the man who'd shot up his house in Golden Valley, a man alone with his anger and hate. Then I thought how lucky I was to have a family awaiting me, how family gives the world a sense of rightness. A few minutes passed before I looked at my watch. I had jobs waiting and no time left for lunch. My cell phone rang, Maura wanting to know why I'd been delayed. I said I was on my way to the next job, "No more than thirty minutes."

I closed the drapes on the way out and locked the door. I stood looking at Katie's well-kept house and thought with any luck a good family would someday make it a home. They'd place their own pictures on the walls and make noise and listen to music. I wanted to believe all that, but when I got home from the other jobs late that night, I believed none of it. I stood stiffly in the threshold and called my family to me. I gazed at each of them, lingering without offering explanation, just looking from face to face, memorizing every feature.

"What's wrong?" Maura asked.

I said, because there was nothing else in me, "Let's go out to dinner."

"You're weird," my daughter said.

"Where are we going, Dad?" my son asked.

Maura looked at me for a moment, then patted my cheek. When we came home from dinner, she poured me a stiff shot of sixteen-year aged Bushmills and sat on my lap. I didn't tell her what I saw or what I did, still haven't, and she hasn't asked. But she knows something is on my mind. I want to tell her, and eventually I will, but I don't yet know how to put into words what I feel. Maybe I'm concerned Maura may judge me for going back inside that house. Ethics and all. I ask myself what I was expecting to find in Katie's journal. A suicide note?

Some elaborated account of what drove her to try it? All I picture is the panel of photographs on the mirror, people so important to an old woman that her next-to-final act was to leave their images behind. Now, I carry pictures of my family, my Irish wife, my half-Irish, half-Hispanic children, in my van. I look at their smiling images. I hold the photos and run my fingers gently over the flat surface. Doing so helps bring purpose to my work and comfort to my days, even the bad ones.

tolerance

It's dusk at the time of year when the sun drops behind Telescope Peak as the full moon rises over Mt. Charleston. Though darkness hasn't yet fallen, the crickets are in full concert. Some evenings, smog from L.A. and the Inland Empire hangs thick on the distant horizon and the sky at sunset seems aflame, but for the last three days summer winds from the south have cleared the air. Now, the sky glistens silver but reflects no image.

Marcie sits on a lawn chair beside Gabe, who's sipping on his last bottle of Coors as they watch the mountains evolve into shadows. The twelve pack he consumes each week is his only indulgence. Tomorrow he'll drive the pickup to work in Pahrump and replenish his stock and buy whatever items from the grocery Marcie writes on her weekly list. By her own admission, she lacks discipline to stick to items on a list, so soon after their moving to the Flats they agreed that she'd write a list of what is needed for the week and give it to him. Those years, when both of them worked, she was free to indulge her spendthrift ways and Gabe never complained, but now she doesn't work and he works only part time, so they, like most all the inhabitants of Rabbit Flats, live on a limited income and every dollar spent has to go for a good purpose.

Marcie reaches over and takes Gabe's hand in both of hers. She kneads his calloused palm and asks if he'll be working in the shed tonight. "You spent most of the day in there."

"We talked about it. It's a hundred eighty dollars. Got to finish it for the Pahrump League of Women Voters by next week."

"Well, I guess. But you can relax for a while, can't you?"

"I am. I think so, anyhow."

She kneads her thumbs in a little deeper. "That feel better?"

"You could do it all night."

"I could, but I won't." She lets go of his hand. "How long do you think it'll take before Marvin fires off a few rounds?"

"Never would suit me."

The temperature hovers just under a hundred degrees, bearable but not comfortable. A westerly breeze promises to cool the desert. Anticipating that, they left the windows and doors to their trailer open in hopes of cutting down power bills. Muffled sounds come from the trailers and manufactured homes scattered about on the dry crust of earth called Rabbit Flats. Gabe and Marcie live in Lot 10, far enough from others that the distorted sounds of music and television coming from neighbors' homes are barely audible. Out here, several miles north of Pahrump, garble of all manner, roosters at dawn, diesel generators in the evening, coyotes at midnight, is something a person lives with. Nearby, the refrain from Bob Seger's "Ship of Fools" tails off. Gabe figures it originated from Ramon's nearby trailer. Ramon has a collection of '70s and '80s rock music that he cycles through each week. Other than Bill Henderson, who lives on the next acre to the west, Ramon's their nearest neighbor.

Gabe and Marcie rarely turn on their CD player or their television. They prefer listening to crickets. They didn't much care for Rabbit Flats five years ago when they first moved into the double-wide Marcie inherited from her Aunt Lola. The old women left her that, three acres of sand and rock, and cats. Though, at first, they resisted the change, having moved from a 2,400-square-foot stucco home in Sommerland, they've since adjusted to their circumstance. Besides the trailer and three acres of land, the will included seventeen thousand dollars. The inheritance came with the caveat that Marcie live in the trailer and care for Lola Means's three cats until all were dead. Marcie resented her aunt's narrow dictum, but she and Gabe were down on their luck at the time. Marcie was recovering from a second back surgery and Gabe felt the squeeze of bills and loss of income when construction collapsed in Las Vegas. Her aunt's death gave them hope.

Mew, the youngest of the cats, was ten when Lola Means died, and Feathers, the oldest, was thirteen. Dog people, Gabe and Marcie had gone through three Labradors since they'd married. Cats, they discovered, live far longer than dogs. And the three in their care have managed to survive despite a band of coyotes that has claimed several other pets in the community over the intervening years.

The serene moment is abruptly interrupted by a flurry of gunfire echoing across the desert, a regular occurrence the residents of Rabbit Flats have come to tolerate.

"Marv's at it," Gabe says.

"Starting a bit early. Hope he's good and drunk. Might otherwise go on into the night. Keep me and the cats up."

Gabe smiles. "Hell, wish I had the money he blows on bullets. We had it, we could move."

"And forfeit the inheritance? And what would we do then? If we're lucky, he'll give it up sometime before midnight."

The door on Bill Harrison's trailer swings open. Bill, their nearest neighbor, stands silhouetted in the doorway as if trying to decide what direction to take. Bill is a born-again who packs a pocket Bible with him everywhere he goes and blesses people whether they want his blessing or not. He looks in Gabe and Marcie's direction and waves.

"I see company," Gabe says. "All I want is that sunset and what remains in this bottle. Some people don't understand peace. Can't stand it when someone else is having some."

"And I wanted a palace on the Riviera, but I got a trailer in Rabbit Flats because my aunt, bless her, didn't move to France and get rich. You be nice if he comes over."

"Let's turn ourselves around and watch the moon rise. Maybe our backs to him will be a hint. I hear he wants to convert his double-wide into a church and build a stick-and-stucco house on a foundation on that plot of earth he calls sacred ground. That's all we need. A bunch of holy rollers and hallelujahs all Sunday morning."

Marcie nods, but her attention is on Bill, who's closed his door and is headed in their direction.

Rabbit Flats is home to some three dozen citizens, their trailers and homes scattered over sixteen hundred acres of valley land in the desert. Like Bill, half the residents are evangelicals, some having been converted by him, others having fled the stresses of Henderson or Las Vegas to join the congregation in Pahrump. One family, the Miltons, moved up from Riverside. On Sunday, the church-goers line up their cars and trucks on the dirt road that leads to the highway, and with Bill's Ford Explorer at the head, they drive in a caravan to the First Congregational Church of the Lord in Pahrump. In between visits to the church, they call on homes of the unconverted and praise the Lord and quote gospel as they condemn sin, booze mostly, but dancing and any kind of joy seem to have a place on their list as well.

Another burst of gunfire rips over the flats.

"Just wanted to enjoy that sky," Gabe says.

"Well, here he comes anyhow. Be nice."

"I should've killed those cats years ago."

Marcie slaps him on the thigh. "Don't ever. My aunt helped us when we needed it. And you love those cats."

"Right, but they don't love me. I need another beer."

Bill places two fingers on his brow and salutes them as he nears their gate. Gabe has built one of the few fences in the area. Once, Marcie stepped out at night and found herself face to face with a male coyote she figured weighed fifty pounds. It snarled at her and she growled back. For a brief moment, the animal gazed at her then, realizing he'd met his match, he turned away and in two strides jumped the four-foot fence. To discourage a repeat of the incident, Gabe lengthened the posts and added a foot of razor wire to the top of the chain link.

"Still drinking, I see." Bill stands at the gate as if waiting for an invitation. "Can I come in?"

Marvin cuts loose with another burst of gunfire.

Bill looks in the direction of the sound. "Man's crazy. Maybe the deputies should look in on his activities."

"Come on in," Marcie says. "Gabe, grab our guest a chair."

Gabe swallows the last gulp of beer, nods, and goes inside the trailer.

"Go ahead and take his chair," Marcie says to Bill. "Gabe can sit on the one he brings."

From inside the trailer Gabe hears her make the offer. "Sure," he mumbles, "take it."

"Thanks." Bill plops himself down beside her.

Marcie says, "Just watching the sun go down."

"You folks still haven't put up a satellite dish?"

"No. Gabe's got no interest in television and I don't miss it. He brings me two books a week from the library in Pahrump. Reads himself when he's not sanding some piece of wood."

"Only one book worth reading," Bill says and pats the shirt pocket.

"Aside from this, my dish gets me fifteen channels of Jesus. You ever listen to Jerry Falwell."

"No."

Carrying a chair from the kitchen, Gabe steps out of the trailer. "I got this for . . . Never mind, I see you're already comfortable."

Bill nods. "Nice lawn chair."

Gabe sets the kitchen chair down so that Marcie sits between the two of them. Bill, a recovering alcoholic and former car salesman, took the "hump to Pahrump," as he calls it, initially moving from Las Vegas to open a brothel, but that deal fell through when his backers, housing investors from Southern California, went upside down on their properties. Bill found a job selling souvenirs and gem rocks in Pahrump the same year he found Jesus. He claims now that spreading the Lord's Word is all life ever really intended for him.

"I heard your aunt was a strong believer?"

"I believe you told us that before," Marcie says.

"A thousand times," Gabe mutters.

Marcie gives Gabe an icy glance. "What can we offer you, Bill? Something to drink? I made some cookies."

"I drank the last of the beer," Gabe says. "Sorry."

"You know I don't drink alcohol."

"Right. Things slip my mind. Hell, I forgot my last birthday until Marcie got all over me for not buying the birthday cake she put on the shopping list. Isn't that right, honey?"

"You did it on purpose." Marcie reaches over and squeezes his thigh.

A silver cast outlines Telescope Peak, but elsewhere the sky has darkened and the stars are out. Another blast of gunfire comes from Marvin's trailer. He lives as a recluse at the far western edge of the community on ten acres, one of which is filled with the hollow shells of cars and trucks he's hauled in, most now stripped of doors, mirrors, radiators, tires, and wheels. He greets people in passing but never lingers to talk. When he's not on a shooting binge, he sits on one or another of the dead cars and plays a guitar, often into the late hours of the night.

Marvin's a continual focus of people's speculation. Some in the community figure him to be a fugitive, some say he's a crazed Vietnam vet, the more romantic insist he must be a defrocked priest or former rock guitarist. His hair's black, but his beard's gray. Because of this, some guess his age at fifty something, others say his mid-sixties. No one knows, because all anyone ever gets out of him is a curt "Hi."

He built a makeshift greenhouse, constructing its roof from windows of the junked cars. Soon after removing windshields and windows, he began shooting bullet holes in the metal carcasses. No one knows for certain, but the citizens of Rabbit Flats say his greenhouse is a cannabis farm. No one dares venture onto his place to confirm his suspicions and the Nye County sheriff's deputies, despite their many forays to his trailer, have never searched the greenhouse. Gabe figures Marvin's crazy behavior is not crazy, but well thought out. What he knows with certainty is that Marvin provides the people in the community with something to occupy their imaginations and take their minds off their otherwise bland lives.

"That man needs God in his life," Bill says.

"Amen to that," Gabe says. "Go on over and give it a shot."

Gracie elbows him. Pink Floyd's "Dark Side of The Moon" plays somewhere in the background, that tune discordant with another song drifting through the air, and sung by a woman whom Gabe doesn't recognize. That music, however, he knows is played by Deanna, the fifteen-year-old who lives with her father, Tanner Jones, a disabled vet from the war in Iraq, who, like Marvin, prefers his own company to that of others.

"What I came over for is to talk a bit about the benefits of the Lord," Bill says.

"What would those be?" Gracie asks.

It's Gabe's turn to elbow her.

"Well, we've researched the laws, and it's possible that if we become a community of believers and say, some men like Gabe became deacons, we could get numerous exemptions. See, I'm—or maybe you heard already—going to build a house and make my trailer into a church. If I can raise the money, I may employ your talents, Gabe. You being a carpenter."

"You can save a lot by buying prefabs. I'd just slow you down." Gabe smiles as he envisions Bill's plan, which he imagines to benefit Bill at the expense of others.

"Why, we can produce key chains and picture frames and do so tax-free if the money goes to the church. You see, my plan is—and

I've got the website and such going–to sell them on the Internet. Now, before you object, think about how many people out here are on fixed incomes. At least half on social security, a few on one welfare program or another. There's that Marianne who's got what? Four kids and no man? Why I–"

"I heard you were visiting her quite a bit," Gabe says, for which he receives a sharp elbow in the side.

"Yes, I *have* been. The Lord's work. But, back to the plan. I figure in time to expand to charm bracelets and necklaces. Stuff with religious meaning somehow, then to get the products on cable television by giving preachers a share of the proceeds. We can operate like the Chinese, you know, in a factory, small scale of course, even assembling souvenirs eventually. Like genuine Indian artifacts. Cut into that market as well."

Marvin fires three rounds this time.

"He's going for the cars again," Gabe says.

"If you consider we can produce and sell everything pretty much tax-free, we can have most of the community earning a good living."

"That sounds not too bad," Gabe says. "What I make working three days a week in Pahrump at a Seven-Eleven is barely enough to pay for our chateau in the Alps. Any chance we could make enough to buy one on the Riviera? Marcie has something like that in mind."

"Stop it, Gabe," she says.

"Okay. I'll leave you two to the discussion and go feed the cats."

As Gabe opens the screen door, Bill asks, "Remember our talk? You ever think about Jesus?"

Gabe does. He thinks of Him in a way Bill never could, imagines a man tooling wood, smoothing and planing a surface, running His hand over the grain, then carving the edge to an even bevel, every detail important, a man seeking the kind of flawlessness all humans who work with their hands should strive for, the kind of perfection that, despite their greatest efforts, they will invariably come up just short of achieving. He pictures Jesus on the cross, blood dripping from His thorny crown, thinking as He hangs in pain, how cruel men are to do this to another like them, and how coarse of them, in their haste to inflict punishment, to make such a crude cross. Surely, they could've found a better carpenter.

"Yeah, Bill. I think about Him." The screen door creaks as he closes it.

As soon as Gabe picks up the cats' dishes, Oscar, Mews, and Feathers come out of their hiding places, circle his ankles, then rub up against him and mew. Though he complains about them, the truth is they've taken to him in a way that they haven't with Marcie, and he's taken to them as well. He eavesdrops on Bill's conversation as he spoons food onto their dishes and sets the cats' bowls down, slowly one at a time so as to squeeze as much time out of the act as possible.

As Bill explains his vision for the future, Gabe finds himself feeling more ill at ease. Bill speaks of tapping into the aquifer beneath the desert floor, of a community growing, the potential of people occupying now unsold acreage, the chance of dividing up existing acres and selling those, all of this if only there were jobs. Bill sees at least one paved street linking all the homes of all residents and someday a school, privately funded and taught by evangelical instructors. Of course, it begins with his church. He'll be ordained, he says, within the month. With un-Christian pride he says that he's getting his online.

Gabe remembers thinking that in coming to Rabbit Flats he'd felt a sense of failure, that he'd lived for no purpose because everything he'd struggled to make his own was gone, first his shop, then their house. For two years he viewed his exile to the desert as punishment, a form of limbo, and wanted nothing more than to leave, return to some civilized place and start over. Then one day when out wandering in the flats he watched a desert tortoise climb the sloping bank of an arroyo, struggling over rock and loose sand. He wanted to go to its aid, but knew in doing so he might cause it to lose the water in its shell that acts as a natural coolant and makes it possible for the lumbering reptile to survive the harsh climate. He watched the tortoise travel that slow steady journey to the rim and when it finally reached level ground, he felt like cheering.

Gabe picks up Mew and snuggles her to his neck. She kneads his shoulder playfully with her claws and begins to purr. He closes his eyes and wonders about ambition, why he didn't have any, at least not the kind that drives men like Bill. All he'd ever wanted was ten-hour days working with his hands, tooling cabinets from hardwood, every line, every corner, every shelf precise. He'd been content with his small cabinetry business in Henderson, a one-man operation, but when the boom hit the Las Vegas Valley in the years just before the Millennium, contractors had little need of one-man shops. As developers gobbled up an ever-shrinking desert, their contractors installed prefab cabinets made on assembly lines in China and Indonesia. Then came the construction bust, real estate collapse, and the recession. The sole remnants of his shop are the tools he keeps in a work shed behind the trailer.

He sits down on the linoleum and Oscar and Feathers climb on his lap. Sometimes they just tolerate him, the way they do Marcie, and sometimes they seem to intuit that he needs the solace they bring him when they curl up on his lap. *Two beers a day*, he thinks, *is not a sin. Watching the sunset is not a sin. Maybe shooting bullets in the air is not a sin. Or growing a little weed.* He sets the cats aside gently and walks to the door. The screen door creaks as he opens it. Marcie and Bill turn in his direction. He listens for music and hears nothing but crickets chirping. Bill speaks to him, something about Gabe giving thought to the plan, but Gabe can't process the words in any meaningful way. Marcie asks if he's feeling down.

"I'm fine," Gabe says.

HE LOOKS TO THE east where the full moon rests above mountain peaks outlined by the glow of neon from Las Vegas where his cousin grinds out nights dealing cards in a casino. There in the turbid dome of light the sky is void of stars. He gazes to the north where stars glitter above Death Valley, a sight he finds comforting. He considers the expression used to describe people's good or bad fortune, the idea of stars being or not being in proper alignment. Stars, he thinks, are never out of alignment. It's people who aren't properly aligned. He's rarely amazed at Marcie's tolerance of others, but his own incipient tolerance requires vast spaces and sunsets and stars. He feels it being threatened and remembers a poem from an eighth-grade class about fences making good neighbors, and realizes that you can't fence out everything and that a fence is the last thing he wants in life.

"Gabe, you sure you're okay?" his wife asks.

"Yeah, I'm sure," he says, but he doubts that even as he says it.

The coyotes will be out soon. They've been passing by the trailer lately. This night he'll go to the work shed and finish the table he started last week. He'll stay up late and watch for the coyotes. If he's lucky, they'll hang around for a time and share some mutual curiosity. Then he'll be fine, at least for the time being, in a world that makes some sense, but he's beginning to wonder if tolerance is a fair tradeoff for serenity.

life is a country western song

Along with cats and movies, country western songs had been Laura's passion. She memorized actors and their roles from most every film produced during the eighties and early nineties, but her real love was reserved for the whiskey-drinking bad boys: Johnny Cash, Merle Haggard, Buck Owens, kings of the middle era of country western music. She'd sing their songs, never missing a word or note. At times, she imagined herself much like the women in those songs–living the hard times, with a hard man, and feeling the heartaches. She'd been tall and ungainly as a girl and didn't date much in high school. Longing as she did for the kind of deep feelings no high-school boy could stitch across her heart, she sought solace in the dream world woven in song, and that eased the pain of her teenage years.

Then two weeks after she turned nineteen, a hazel-eyed, square-jawed, bourbon-drinking man, a man half a head taller than most and too old for her, singled her out of a crowd and threaded his way across a packed dance floor. He introduced himself as Brent Castle and asked her to dance. She shook her head and cast her gaze on the floor where the toes of his cowboy boots reflected light from the stage. He kneeled down on one knee and smiled up at her, a broad flashy smile, and said that she'd already broken his heart when he first saw her and it would be unkind of her to break it twice in one night. He eased himself to his feet, took her hand and placed his other on the small of her back as he guided her out onto the dance floor. They danced the two-step, him twirling her easily and pulling her into his arms, every step, every move so fluid she felt as if she were on a sail-boat gliding across crystal waters, not a remnant of her school-girlish gracelessness in evidence. When finally, after a half-dozen songs they left the dance floor, she was giddy and asked if he was a man who liked cats.

"Love them," he said.

For nearly a month following that first meeting, they dated, dining out, dancing afterward, mostly the country two-step. He claimed he was rich and had earned his wealth as a cattle broker purchasing and selling beeves from Idaho to the north and Arizona to the south and had recently sold his horse ranch in Montana. She sometimes imagined him one of the romantic heroes she'd seen on the big screen, but more often, one of the rugged outlaw men who sang country western songs. At last, her life seemed no longer a dream. She was deep inside her own country western ballad.

One night, as they waited for dessert, he laid two one-way tickets to Nicaragua on the table. He said a beach house awaited them on the Atlantic-side and he promised to make her happy in ways she could only imagine. They'd live in modest luxury. He always carried large sums of cash with him and spent money freely, so she didn't doubt him. But there was the question of her cat, Mittens. Could she have a horse? she asked. Of course. Could she take her cat along? He said that, though he was a man who liked cats, she'd have to leave hers behind. They would find a new one, a black one with white paws, and name it Boots. His saying that made her heart rise in her chest.

That night she had sex for the first time.

The following evening, as she sat debating whether to go off with her man or stay with her cat, the phone rang, a call from Kathy, her best friend, who told her to switch on the evening news. There, on the screen, was his mug shot, his hair tousled, his eyes squinting at the camera. A local Reno news announcer offered up undeniable proof of her lover's deception. His real name was Oscar Neiman. He was a fugitive wanted in four states, thirty-eight years old, and not the twenty-eight he'd claimed. He had a wife and son in Colorado.

As Kathy tried to console her over the phone, Laura broke out in uncontrollable sobbing. She worried that she was pregnant. In the end, she wasn't. Despite his deception or maybe because of it, the man wanted for a string of bank robberies had broken her heart. After that evening she never talked of him to anyone. She heard from him only once, a handwritten letter postmarked from the federal penitentiary in Fort Leavenworth, Kansas. In it he said he regretted lying to her, and that after they'd made love, he realized that even if he hadn't been arrested, he couldn't continue with the lie. He said that his feelings had been sincere and ended the letter by saying that he didn't expect her to write, though it would be nice if she did.

She never wrote to him, but she kept his letter with his prisoner number on it, and he remained in the recesses of her mind, emerging whenever she found herself attracted to a new suitor. A year and a half later, still on the rebound, she married Ronald. A hardworking carpenter, he was a steady husband who wanted a family and who never complained about their sharing the bed at night with Mittens. He also proved ambitious. Three years into the marriage he passed the test to become a contractor and started his own business. She worked as a secretary at a bank. To the world outside, theirs seemed an ideal marriage. No one knew that her fugitive's face was the one she looked for in crowded casinos or the man she hoped to find when she hurried to catch up with a tall man on a busy sidewalk, one who walked with a long-legged stride like her fugitive.

Ronald and her parents were delighted when she became pregnant with a son. They named the boy Lonnie and she pretended to be happy, believing her life was not a country western song and that happiness, at best, was an illusion and that she could hope for nothing better. But, whenever she was alone with her thoughts, the fugitive seemed always somewhere in every room, sometimes a shadow cast by a lamp, sometimes a sound in the bowels of the house. When she and Ronald made love, her fugitive's handsome outlaw face was the fantasy that carried her over the edge. He was on call as well whenever she masturbated, an act that became more frequent as her marriage entered the second decade.

The only thing Ronald ever objected to with any frequency was her playing "Folsom Prison Blues," which she did at least three times a day. When he complained and asked why that song, she said, "Because it's true."

"True?" he shouted once. "A man who kills someone in Reno is sent to Carson City? Turn it off. It's a lie!"

Eighteen years into the marriage, Ronald confessed to having an affair with a younger woman. Upon hearing this, the only thing Laura felt was relief. Thinking that, given the circumstances, her parents and son would understand it, she filed for divorce. A month later the divorce was granted. Two years after the divorce, Lonnie went off to college. Mittens had died. Laura replaced him with Nick and Nora, named after the odd but sophisticated characters from *The Thin Man*, a classic movie she'd seen at a film festival.

Alone with her cats, memories of her fugitive, and the Internet, she began her search. She discovered that after serving ten years, Oscar Neiman had been paroled, his sentence reduced because of good behavior. From there, he disappeared. During those long interludes when she searched, she felt the intervening years had been a continuum of dullness, not just a continuum but a dream of dullness. The one thing that seemed real in her life was the dark-haired liar who'd drawn her into his fiction. As she plowed through the data on the net, she was certain he was thinking of her. He had to be. She had little luck tracking him down, and for a time she set the search aside, content to believe he'd escaped to Nicaragua and was walking the beach barefoot while sipping claret, a glass of which she kept at hand whenever she sat before the keyboard.

Two months later, she renewed her search, typing in his identity in every variant she could imagine, the three aliases she found he'd used while on the lam, his parents' names, and his description, sixty-eight, six-feet-three-inches tall, two hundred pounds, hazel eyes. Using the alias of Charity101, she sent out woman-seeking-man notices on every Internet social site, requiring that he must be a convicted bank robber and a man who likes cats. She requested that respondents send pictures of themselves. The week following her posting, she received sixty-two answers, twelve from men still on the run for their crimes; five from men still in prison; three from lesbians, and a transgender person who anticipated being a man within a year. One supposed bank robber asked if she was a cougar looking for a young stud.

She screened their answers carefully and with hope. After evaluating the results, none of which were promising, she typed in some additional strings, first revealing more information about herself—a woman who once owned Mittens—then a little more about her fugitive, a man who bought airline tickets to Nicaragua. Though not a mathematician, she was certain she'd reduced the odds to five or six out of the billions of men on the planet.

Three weeks later, Laura came home from the bank where she was now a loan officer and turned on her computer. A message awaited her on Facebook from Galveston702, who requested that she friend him. She recognized the numbers as the last three of Oscar's prisoner number. She accepted the invitation and read the message he'd left her. "It's not your real name," the message began, and it ended with, "Is Mittens still alive?" Overjoyed, she typed in, "No, Mittens died several years ago. What is my real name then?" When she didn't get an immediate reply, she asked why he didn't have his picture posted and if he knew the name of a club on Kietzke Lane in Reno. Her heart beating, she hit Enter.

Two days passed without receiving a reply, and for those two days she suffered through eight hours at the bank and another six at night waiting for the message board to light up. She was called in to see the vice-president and explain why she hadn't approved his nephew's loan. Then she bungled the closing date on a business loan. Two mistakes in two days, one more than she'd made in nine years as a loan officer. She stumbled into the house, fed the cats, uncorked a fresh bottle of claret, poured herself a glass, and sat at the kitchen table staring at the room where her computer waited her atop an oak desk. She wondered how she'd become the kind of person who gave herself over to a brief moment from the past. Could anything she now did reverse the heartache of a nineteen-year-old? And what would she gain even if he answered? He was old now, and she still had the juices of youth flowing in her.

A half hour passed before she pulled herself up from the table and poured herself a fresh glass of wine. She sat down before the screen and tentatively pressed the On button. The screen bloomed to life, displaying an array of options. The sheer number of choices struck a chord of despair. Hers, it seemed, were two—to continue sitting or to leave. But she couldn't force herself away from the machine. She sipped her wine and opened her email. The page listed a few messages mixed with a lot of spam. Near the middle of the list was a notice that Galveston702 had left a message. She read the others first, one from a man in Nicaragua who asked if she wasn't really an FBI agent, another from a man in Port Arthur who wanted to arrange a meeting in Las Vegas, and another who said he was the man she was looking for, even if he wasn't the man she was trying to find.

Finally, she opened the message from Galveston702. It read, "I can't remember the name of the club, but it was at Kietzke and

Moana. You wore tight jeans, a burgundy tank top, and high heels. You had ID that claimed you were twenty-two. And you're Laura," facts that only her fugitive would know. She read the letter twice again and stared at the screen for several minutes, thinking, *at last*, the one constant in her thoughts for all those years. Then she typed, "Where are you?"

For the next week in the evening they passed messages back and forth, revealing what lives they'd had since his arrest. He wrote about his years in prison, the men he shared a cell with, food they ate, nights he lay sleepless and longing for her. He wondered in his messages what their lives might have been had he not been captured. The beach house was real, he insisted, not some fantasy he'd concocted. Yes, he'd lied about his age, but what was age after all? Do people notice themselves age day to day?

She wrote back, slowly revealing intimate parts of her life: her son's name, the way her cats would gang up on her when she wasn't paying them adequate attention, how Ronald's new wife took advantage of him. The weather was often included as a watermark of the past. She asked if he remembered how quickly winter came in Reno and how short spring was and it was April now and that was the month he'd been arrested. She confessed that she thought about him whenever she had sex with her former husband.

"Did you," he wrote, "love him?" She thought about that question for two days before answering, "At times, at first." He wrote back that probably most people love that way, that people put conditions on love. He said he loved her all those years and still did, that it had comforted him in moments when he was about to abandon all hope. "Real love," he wrote, "doesn't have an expiration date like a label on milk and medicine."

The affairs of her small life took on new color and significance. Every little detail began to matter. Though preoccupied with what message might be awaiting her in the evening, Laura did her daily work efficiently. Whereas before she'd looked forward mostly to lunch breaks, now interviewing clients and filling out forms gave her a sense of purpose. She began wearing lipstick again, something she'd rarely done since her divorce. For years, she'd driven to and from work in a fog-like state. Now she noted details she'd missed. She'd walked for lunch from the bank down Virginia Street every weekday noon for over twenty years and hadn't noticed that Harold's Club was no longer there and the Prima Donna was gone. Maybe she'd heard about these events, but now she was aware not just of them, but of more, so much more.

A month later her requests to meet with him became demands. "We must," she wrote, "or I'll have to stop this." He wrote that she had to be patient, that he wasn't in any position to travel, even though he wanted desperately to see her. "I'll travel to you," she wrote. "I have vacation days stored up. Tell me where. Please." Though she implored him to tell her, he didn't give her his address or name the city he lived in, said that he wasn't in a position to do so.

"What are you in a position to do?"

"For now," he wrote, "just write. I live for your messages, just as I lived on your memory while in prison."

The words "live for" played on her mind, those and a rising sense of incertitude. Is he ill? Is he married? Is he in another prison? Questions shadowed her days. Sometimes she considered cutting off communication with him, thinking that in doing so, she could spur him into action.

As she and Galveston702 reinforced their online relationship, the messages from others interested in her poured in, a number that grew to nearly a thousand. The few she bothered to read ranged from the odd to the outlandish. One claimed he was a man who preferred his cats medium rare. Another said he was a man who loved cats almost as much as robbing banks. Click. Delete. Go to Galveston702. Press. Her fingers repeated the process involuntarily.

Then he stopped messaging her. The days compiled into a week, then two, then three. Her travel from home to work and back became a blur again. She hurried home in the evenings, never thinking to eat or even to pour a glass of wine. The first week she felt distressed, but at the end of three weeks she was numb. Then in late May, Ronald called to say that Lonnie had a girlfriend he was bringing home to Reno at the end of the semester to meet his parents.

"It must be serious," Ronald said.

"Yes, it must be," she said, but she was thinking of her own situation.

She and Ronald and his new wife, Emma, met the couple at the airport and took them to dinner. Lonnie and his new girl held hands and talked nervously the entire meal. They discussed going to graduate school and traveling through Europe on bicycles. Their eyes sparkled as they described how they'd met in a Shakespeare class, one they'd expected to hate, but instead found themselves enraptured by the way the professor revealed Shakespeare's understanding of human ways. Laura saw in the young couple what she'd once tasted, what she now longed for.

Because Emma's grown daughter and two grandchildren lived in Ronald's house, the couple stayed with Laura. At night, though they tried to be discreet, the sounds of their love-making woke her and sent her to the computer, where she sent message after message and played free cell as she waited for any reply. But Galveston702 remained a ghost she couldn't summon.

Matters got no better after Lonnie and his girlfriend left. Laura's hours in front of the screen offered no hope. Galveston702 had vanished from the virtual world, just as he had from her nineteen-year-old self. It was late autumn and the first snow had come when the screen lit up with a message from him. In her excitement, she deleted the message. She restored it and read it through once, then again.

"We apologize if this has been an inconvenience to you. Our son is a paraplegic. He lives on the computer and we discovered he's been carrying on this . . . We don't know. Anyhow, he won't be bothering you any longer. We told him to stop."

She stared at the screen. It made no sense. Where, she wondered, did someone's son get the details that only her fugitive would know? And the names of his cell mates and the description of the food. Facts that couldn't be made up. How much time passed, she didn't know, but she kept staring even as the screen went blank. She came out of her daze when she heard Nick and Nora mewing at her ankles. She looked down. Nick flicked his tail. Nora jumped up into her lap. She petted Nora, then set her back on the floor, stood, and walked mechanically to the kitchen where she opened two cans of cat food and scooped the contents into bowls.

The next morning before she went to work, Laura sat at the computer. She had to know what seemed completely unknowable. She asked that the parent of Galveston702 please explain how his son knew what he knew. The hours of the day seemed to blister, swelling painfully without relief in sight. A second early storm came and darkened the street outside the bank. Business was slow and she dwelled on the painful mystery of her cyber-suitor. Surely, there's an answer. But she found no explanation in anything logical.

It was snowing when she pulled into her driveway that evening. Nick and Nora waited on the kitchen counter. They jumped to the floor and gathered at her feet, a greeting that once gave her joy, but now added to her despair. She sat on the tile, legs splayed, and invited them onto the skirt of her dress.

"I'm sorry," she said. She wasn't sure what she meant in saying it. The cats stared at her. She looked off, pondering how she'd come to this point of her life. She felt like crying, but wasn't sure what she would be crying over, so she didn't. Eventually, she rose and fed the cats. Then she sat in the darkened living room and turned on the television. She flipped from channel to channel, each time pressing the advance button faster and faster as if to confuse the device. The screen sent flickering shadows on the wall.

After turning off the TV, she went to her closet, shrugged out of her dress, and slipped on a pair of jeans and a tee-shirt.

She feared what awaited inside the guts of her computer where letters of the alphabet were digitally stored and somehow transformed into messianic scripture for the confused, the lonely, and the needy. Here, letters became more than symbols to be cobbled into mere words. Reluctantly, she walked into the small unlit room that housed her machine and pressed the power button. The screen illuminated the walls. She bent over the keyboard, typed in a password, and moved the mouse in until the prompt was on the Open Messages button. She clicked on a message sent by reneneiman3 at an AOL address. It began in a formal tone. "Dear Laura, you deserve an explanation." The writer apologized again and began an account of what happened: "Oscar Neiman was my husband's father. I'm sorry to inform you he passed away. He left behind a diary. Our son somehow found it. Now that we've read through it, we realize this must be painful for you. Forgive him. He's lonely and he thought he was making you happy."

She turned off the computer, went to the closet again, and stripped for a bath. She paused in front of the mirror. What was age? She saw no nineteen-year-old in the mirror, just someone who was familiar to her, someone over the years she had come to know and not know. How could the woman in the mirror have become a storehouse for pain?

She didn't sleep well that night or for the next week and she didn't turn on the computer until Saturday. Each day had been an exercise in dullness and routine, interrupted only by the pain that lodged itself in her mind and found its way to her chest. She hadn't heard from her son in weeks and thought he might have left her a message on his Facebook page, the only way he now communicated with her and others. First, she opened her email account. She'd pretended it was urgent because others certainly were concerned about her. She found precisely what she'd both hoped for and hoped she wouldn't find–a series of messages from Galveston702.

She opened the first. It read, "I miss you." She deleted it. The next said, "I won't quit." She deleted it. "I'm eating ice-cream and thinking of you." She deleted that one as well. They went on, some forty in all– "I'm here. Still here. Wondering if you're okay." And the last one said, "Tell me what I can do to get you to answer."

She typed, "Nothing," and hit the Send button.

A reply came within seconds. "See? But you answered."

"Stop it," she typed.

"Never. I'm here till the end of time or until I'm tired or I have to clean out the wax in my ears. Tell me what you've been doing with yourself. I've been concerned."

She smiled and wrote that she'd arranged two loans, had a BLT for lunch, and fielded a few problems for customers. She sent that and waited for his reply.

"You work too hard and probably need a vacation. I'd like to meet you someday, say in Guatemala?"

She pressed a Johnny Cash into the CD player and turned up the volume as the beat triggered the mood.

"Do you still have the beach house?"

The room glowed around her. Nick and Nora curled up near her feet. "Folsom Prison Blues" came to life. She clutched the mouse and waited, imagining as she did a man held prisoner on the other side of time and distance, a man thinking of her, a man of indeterminate age, a bank robber, a captured fugitive, his heart as hungry as hers, his soul deep as a cowboy ballad. She wanted to read of his life in prison, every detail he'd withheld. And she had to ask if he truly liked cats. *That*, she knew, was important information. The message board popped up, a message from his address. She pressed the left control on her mouse and began smiling. It didn't matter what he wrote, only that he did.

in the end

Stepping out of the parking-lot elevator, Carl caught sight of his blurred reflection in the metal doors: shoulders slumped, head bowed, the image of a crushed man. For a moment, he considered going back and pleading his case, but decided any appeal to the old man would be useless. As were all his dad's decisions, this one was irrevocable. He'd seen the old man go cold that way before, at business meetings, at company parties, at baseball games.

He crossed the parking lot, his mind a windstorm of doubt and worry. Lately the budget had gotten tight at home because the kids' college tuition had all but drained the money well. Now, Carl was stuck with wondering how far two weeks' severance and ten days' vacation pay would stretch. Was it the same pittance any lowly account rep would receive if given the boot? A month? That, along with their savings, would keep Marie and him afloat for three, maybe four months. No matter, it was done. What was left for him to do now was make contacts, send out résumés and wait. Gina would never press charges, and even with rumors of sexual harassment circulating, surely someone would hire him. Surely, one of his connections would come through after all his years in the business.

But that was days ahead. Right now, he had to figure out how to break the news to Marie. How would he explain to her what'd happened? How would she take it? She'd be mad, sure, but eventually she'd get over her anger. The adjustment would just take time. He tried to bolster himself by weighing in her age and general situation—forty-two and pampered. She hadn't held down a job for sixteen years. How many options did she have? Him. Yeah, he was pretty much it. Okay, the marriage wasn't perfect, but it'd survived his affair with Inge eight years before. More was at stake then. Back then, the kids had been in their early teens so the threat of a divorce came and went without their knowledge of it and was never again to be mentioned by her. This present circumstance would cause a crisis, sure, but not one that could break up their marriage.

If she could handle all that, surely they could work their way through his being fired. He felt his confidence rekindle as he neared the executive parking spaces, but when he reached the one that read "Reserved for Carl Peirce, Jr.," what confidence he'd mustered walking to his car began to wane. Loser, he thought. He'd only once before thought of himself as a loser. Now the idea took hold. He hadn't just lost a job. He'd lost a title and parking privileges. "Jesus, is this what it's like?" he muttered. "Is it?"

He unlocked the Mercedes, his eight-hundred-dollar-a-month piece of luxury on four low-profile tires, his emblem of arrival, and sat momentarily, his fingers firm around the leather-covered steering wheel. The car would have to go. Hell, he thought, replacing tires on it alone will be too much to afford. But he loved the car. So did Marie. His guts knotted and his mouth went dry as once again he imagined the pain he was facing in explaining matters to her, a moment that loomed too close. What will her reaction be to hearing he'd been fired? Will she cry? Be angry? Both maybe? Or will she stare, her eyes blank and dry, as she had when years ago he'd confessed his affair? That silent staring would be the worst.

He started the engine, looked in the rearview mirror and caught a glimpse of his eyes, puffy, pale-blue, spider lines at the edges. He'd not cried since he was twelve and had muffed an easy out at first base, which cost his team a spot in the Little League World Series. What had his dad thought of the tears Carl had shed an hour ago along with his pleading for another chance? Of his promises not to repeat that kind of mistake? Jesus, was he wrong to expect a little understanding? Gina was always friendly, often smiling at him as if to invite his attention. He mistook that as an interest in him that went beyond the workplace. His dad should have understood. Understood and forgiven. After all, he was the man's only son. Even if errors weren't reversible, they were forgivable.

Carl backed slowly out of the parking space. A horn honked. He stabbed the brake pedal to avoid being hit from the right side. He glimpsed Gina in the driver's seat of her BMW. His dad probably rewarded her with a day off with pay. *Gina*, he thought, *another mistake. No, an error.* She glared at him. He saw no point in glaring back.

Traffic was thin on the freeway. He turned up the volume on the radio and listened to a scientist being interviewed about climate change. "The Arctic Shelf," the man said, "has been melting for two decades. The seas will gradually rise . . ." just as the sea was rising around him, not a gradual shift, but one sudden and unmerciful. *I know something about that*, he thought.

The road ahead was littered with strips of black rubber from a blowout. He switched lanes to avoid hitting the serpent-like shreds. A car sat stranded on the right side of the freeway. He felt oddly pleased that someone else was having a bad day, even if it paled in comparison to the one he was having. What the hell, share the misery. What was it called, that feeling of satisfaction for someone else's misfortune? Schadenfreude? Yes. Was Gina experiencing her own sense of it right now? Over the span of his forty-four years how many times had he taken pleasure at another's ill fortune? A golden guy sailing smoothly through other people's rough waters.

By the time he'd rounded the Spaghetti Bowl interchange headed toward Summerlin, he'd invented and discarded a half dozen lies. Not lies, he thought, reasoned excuses. Too much stress on the job. His actions had been misinterpreted. His dad had long before thought he wasn't up to the task and hadn't told him. The traffic ahead slowed. He remembered when getting trapped in a snarl of traffic seemed his biggest complaint in life.

Well, he'd downsized before when the kids left for college. From a sprawling four-thousand-square-foot house to one with thirty-one-hundred square feet that backed up to the golf course. Marie insisted that she needed a house of some size. After all, she had family that visited occasionally and friends she entertained regularly. Nearly four hundred grand when he bought it, it was now worth a hair over three hundred grand if he could even sell it. No matter, it would have to go along with his club membership, his Harley, and the F-250–and Marie would have to downsize from her Volvo SUV to a compact of some kind.

Downsizing, he mused–his penalty for making an error in judgment. He thought about his golfing buddies who took it in the shins when the economy tanked. They'd played the real estate market and lost at it. Carl saw a spark of hope. He'd call Efrain and see if he was up to shooting a round of golf. Just a year ago, Efrain had asked Carl to come to work for his food distributorship. Carl didn't know a lot about wholesale foods, but a few of his accounts had been pubs that served food and he knew chefs who might do business with him. Sure, they'd play a round and he'd bring it up, a job–casually, like it was no big deal.

He wondered if his losing the Athena account had played a role in his dad's decision. But the bar supply business was competitive and Las Vegas was a cutthroat market. Sure, he'd forgotten an order for a new beer tap at the bar on Tropicana, but he'd taken the hit on his paycheck and at bonus time he'd gotten none. Merely an oversight. Didn't he send Andy, his top rep, out to make amends? Though it had taken six months, Carl got the account back. That didn't matter to the old man. Clear your desk out, his dad had told him. Cold as the stainless-steel ice-makers they sold.

At least his dad had promised to keep the kids in college and pay their tuition.

Marie's SUV was gone. He pulled into the driveway and shoved the gear shift into park. Did she know already? Had one of the sales reps called and told her? By now he was certain the whole staff, from executives to the men who loaded the trucks, knew. He decided to give his fall from grace a title. The Fall of the Golden Guy. *Maybe*, he thought, *this wouldn't have happened if the economy hadn't sunk as it had.*

"We'll move," he said. He wondered where. And do what?

Inside, he dialed Efrain's cell phone. Efrain picked it up on the fourth ring.

"Hey, Eff," Carl said. "I've got the afternoon free. How about a quick eighteen?"

"I'm bombed, buddy. Maybe Saturday. No, wait. Can't do. Wife's got plans."

Carl didn't have an alternative in mind, so he got to the point. "Eff, you remember that job, that account rep job you offered me?"

"Account rep?"

"Yeah."

"Kind of. What about it? You got someone in mind?"

"Yeah, me. I'm ready for something new. I mean, it's like you said, where am I going to go with my old man? He uh–"

"Hey, pal, I got to go. Call me about golf later. Maybe next week. And listen, we just laid off two reps. You may want to stick it out with your situation for now."

"Sure, yeah. I'll call. Bye." He lowered the receiver and stared at the phone thinking of who else he might call. Golf turned a lot of business. He came up with no one who'd be interested in an afternoon round of golf or who'd consider hiring him.

He turned on the computer in the bedroom he'd converted into an office. The rest of the house was hers. This room, its desk and desk chair, a leather recliner and an entertainment center were all his. Marie had confirmed it by putting a carved wooden sign above the door that read "Man Cave. Ask before entering." Spread over the walls were pictures of his son and daughter, many taken during their years playing soccer. Jared had been an average player and had quit playing at age fourteen, but Emily had been a whiz on the soccer field. "My star," Carl would proclaim to her after each game. He'd hoped she'd get a college scholarship, but only two offers came and those weren't to prestigious colleges. On the shelves on either side of the 42-inch flat screen sat her trophies. How would she take his fall?

He didn't want to think about the immediate future. Or the past, but the past crept into the present as it was wont to. If he could fix matters, fix his life, how far would he have to go back? How many bad choices to contend with? He consoled himself by saying others had made worse choices and survived. He turned his attention to the computer screen, thinking he'd update his resume and realized that he'd not added anything to it since going to work for his dad. What would he write? Supervised five account reps? Managed to lose two, no, three accounts.

He shook his head and looked at the screen and then, maybe because it had long been in the periphery of his thoughts, he typed in "horse property nevada arizona utah," and pressed Search. Ever since he was nine, he'd wanted a horse. That was when his best friend Christian Bosley had let him ride a pinto mare around the Bosleys' riding arena. Though Carl had pleaded for years for a horse of his own, his dad had said no and had even forbidden him to ride any at the Bosley place. "Too dangerous," his old man had said, "save yourself for baseball." A horse was one of the few things Carl Jr. had been denied, one he'd also denied himself as an adult. He wondered what wants his own son had that he'd never expressed. He'd often lavished praise on his daughter, his star, but couldn't recall ever praising Jared? Boys were supposed to have confidence.

More than three million hits flashed up on the screen. He deleted Nevada and Utah from the string of words and waited. He noticed a remote ranch for sale off Route 66 near the town of Seligman and clicked on it. Details describing the place were thin. It had a well and solar power, a small stucco house and horse stalls on twenty-two acres. He imagined what it would be like, all that space, no traffic.

He heard the front door open and shut, footsteps coming toward the room. He turned and called out to Marie.

She stopped at the open door and knocked on the wall. "Permission to come in?"

"Granted," he said, playing along with the game she'd created.

She stood in the doorway and leaned her hip into the jamb. Fresh from a workout, wearing shorts and a halter top, she looked vibrant and healthy, much younger than her years. She turned her head slightly and winked. "What's up, big guy? Why are you home?"

No matter how he phrased it, the story would be as painful for him to tell as it would be for her to hear. Why hurry into bad news? he thought. He shrugged. "I needed a break from the stress."

She walked over, stood at his shoulder and looked at the computer screen. "I see you're looking at horse property? What now?"

"Oh, just thinking about someday retiring."

She narrowed her eyes. Marie was three years younger than he. She'd already had what she called "touchup work." It didn't seem to have made her younger nearly so much as it made her almost a stranger in his eyes, especially the Botox that made her lips look like miniature inflated tires. On the other hand, five days a week doing aerobics and weights at the gym had preserved the rest of her pretty well. Didn't he take pride pointing that out to his buddies as they downed a few at the nineteenth hole?

"Horses?" she said. "Too much work. That's no retirement. Besides, we're young yet."

"Just planning ahead."

"Don't you think you might ask me before you start making horse plans?"

"Right. Sorry, I wasn't thinking."

"Let's go to Delveccio's tonight. I'm not up to cooking."

He looked her up and down. "You look really . . . healthy."

She smiled. "Horses? I'm going to shower." She blew him a kiss and left.

He sat thinking. All he had to do was lay out the truth, because ultimately it was what they both had to live with. Still, he wondered if Gina had set him up, if all of her friendliness and what seemed to be flirtation hadn't been a ploy. Yes, he'd grabbed her by the waist and pulled her to him and tried to kiss her. Yes, she'd said, "Don't." Yes, he'd been aggressive. But these things, he assured himself, were never really one-sided. After all, she'd once smiled when he gave her a hug after she'd helped close a bar account. Hadn't she lingered in his arms? Or had she? Was it merely his misperception?

A random thought flashed in his mind. That game, the grounder he'd muffed, allowing the winning run to score. The blame all on his shoulders. His dad, the team's sponsor, had been, as always, in the stands watching. Afterward, and on the drive home, his dad had said nothing about the blown play, nothing to console him or rebuke him. The game had never again been mentioned, and the next year his dad had dropped his sponsorship of the team and Carl gave up baseball. Had his dad looked for failure in him thereafter? Was Gina the opportunity his dad had been waiting for all these years? Was it a long-awaited moment to finally rebuke him?

He heard the shower go off and stood from the desk with a new sense of resolve. He had to tell Marie eventually. So, do it now. He looked at Emily's trophies and then at a picture of Jared holding a soccer ball to his chest. He realized as he looked at his boy's picture that he'd withheld praise from Jared back then because the boy hadn't earned any. But his son had since earned honors in college. Still, Carl hadn't praised him. Had he expected too much? Is that the lesson he'd learned from his own dad, a man who'd built a business from the ground up, a self-made millionaire? Carl remembered the encouraging words from Christian Bosley's father telling him that he was a natural rider, that he was born to ride a saddle.

He keened his ear to hear signs of Marie. No sound at all. Since the kids had gone off to college, the house was too often silent. Other than at night as they lay beside one another, the only time he was aware of her was when they ate meals or when she entertained. Had they become strangers sharing space? Is that why she needed a big house? To avoid him? What role did his affair play in it?

He gave her a few minutes to dry off and dress, then went to their bedroom. She was seated at the vanity brushing her hair.

She looked at his reflection in the mirror and shook her head. "Did you find your ranch, cowboy?"

"No."

"Well, there are many years ahead and ranges to roam. You know Gala. She owns three horses. She boards them. You can always do that. I mean, if you're serious."

"You wouldn't want to live out in the open? You know, get away from all this?"

"No. Where'd that come from?"

He licked his lips and thought matters might go better if he could hold her and maybe they could make love and talk afterward as they had in the early years of their marriage. He could slip it into the conversation. *You're a coward*, he thought. *Just tell her.* "I lied about coming home to get away from the stress."

She turned and looked at him. "I knew that. You play hooky from work to play golf about once a month. I just figured you couldn't find anyone to play with."

"That's not the case. I got . . . There's something else." He thought how pathetic he must appear, just as he'd appeared when his dad told him to clear out his office.

"So? What's going on?"

He rubbed his forehead, then blurted, "Dad fired me."

She grinned. "Sure he did."

"Really."

He leaned against the wall. She aimed the brush at him as if it were a gun. She didn't speak, just studied him. The silence built slowly as the truth of what he'd said sunk in, for her, for him. Then she asked the inevitable question, the one he'd feared.

"Why? What did you do?"

"There's this woman. You met her at the Christmas office party. Gina McPearson. The redhead. Remember?"

"She's not a real redhead. Anyone could see . . . Wait, don't tell me you had an affair? I don't want to hear that."

"No. She complained."

"Complained?"

"About me. Said that I made advances."

Marie's gaze was unwavering. It was hard for him to look at her, but he did.

"Did you? Did you make advances?"

"She threatened to sue."

Marie continued to stare at him, fear and anger in her eyes at first, then they went blank, just as they had when he'd confessed to his affair.

"Carl, did you? Did you make advances? Did you do that?"

"Yes. I mean, she invited it."

She slumped down in the recliner and looked at the ceiling. "God, you should know better. Your dad fired you? I mean, he fired you?"

He looked for something in her eyes and what he saw now seemed, not like hate exactly, but more the gaze of a wounded and desperate animal.

"Yeah, he did."

"What did he say?"

"That I'd disappointed him."

"That's all?"

"He said he'd pay the kids' tuition."

She shook the brush at him. "No. What did he say?"

"That a lawsuit for sexual harassment could destroy the business. Matters were tough enough as it was."

She leaned forward, let the brush drop to the floor and cupped her hands over her eyes. He knew it would be a mistake to try and comfort her. He remained dead still until her sobs grew too loud to bear, then he went to the family room bar and poured a shot of scotch. He didn't swallow it as he'd planned to, merely took a sip and thought about the fact that his dad had never before expressed disappointment. He must have felt it, but in the end his last words were, "You're through."

Carl looked at the Azoulay silkscreen on the wall, the Italian brass dining table with the glass top, the bowl of fragile ceramic apples—ornaments, rewards of the good life. All of it too easy, all of it a lie, none of it truly earned, at least not in the way that honest praise is earned. He wondered how Marie would take his apology, wondered how his son would, wondered if he could earn his way back into their hearts.

He sat on the bar stool and swirled the drink twice before he downed it. He thought of the horse he'd ridden, the idea of having his own and saw it as a lie. Then he buried his head in his arms and his chest convulsed. He gathered himself together enough to shout out to her. "I'll get a job! We may have to let the cars go, but I'll make it up to you. We'll keep the house. Don't worry."

She didn't respond.

He looked back at the hallway that led to the bedroom. "I'm sorry," he shouted. He knew it sounded feeble. He said more softly, "I'm terribly sorry."

He braced himself and stood as Marie entered.

She used the back of her hand to wipe away the traces of tears, then gazed at him as if trying to decide if she recognized him from some distant past. "It's not the job, Carl. Or the cars or any of this."

"No. No, not the job."

He sensed unspoken words swirling about the hollow space that separated them. In the end, the words would be about his failures and those whom he'd disappointed—her, his dad, his son, Gina. He couldn't bear to look at his wife, the pretty and charming woman he'd felt he was entitled to. He gazed down at his fingers so rigidly entwined they were numb and waited for her to speak. He wanted to feel her hurt, wanted it to be his as well, and whatever came from that he didn't want it to be easy because easy was just another lie he'd be telling himself. A minute passed in silence, then two. He opened his hands, looked across the room where she stood, arms folded, back pressed stiffly against the wall, eyes trained on him, and he nodded.

divas

Cliff steps back. He's somehow painted a praying nun and not the vision of the woman kneeling on stage who drifts in his mind, both solace and a faint ache. He squeezes a patch of black onto his palettte knife and smears a diagonal swath down the canvas, then repeats that from the top right. Take up a hobby you're passionate about, the cardiologist had advised. Maybe he should tell the healer the hobby isn't working?

He cleans his brush and palette knife, then places them in his paint box. He sets the palette atop the box, sits on the stool, and sips on a glass of Malbec. The final refrain of Desdemona's aria pours from the stereo in the family room. Cliff imagines her in white stretching out on her bed, fated to die at the hands of her jealous husband. Maybe, he thinks, if he had a bit of Otello's passion, he might produce a painting that at least resembled art.

Where did it go, the mania that compelled him at sixteen to spend hours locked in his bedroom sketching with pencil or charcoal, his mother shouting through the door for him to come out? That she was leaving for work and he'd have to feed his three younger brothers and hyperkinetic sister. Then there was never enough time to feed his passion. Now no one's knocking at the door. No one's telling him he's wasting his time, except himself.

Desdemona's dead, lost to Otello's rage. Cliff goes to the family room and turns off the stereo. Otello's impassioned pleas anger him. After listening to the opera in full, he bought a copy of *Othello* hoping to better understand the Moor's fall from grace, but reading Shakespeare merely raised more and darker questions. Does Iago exist in our heads? Are we waiting to be seduced by villainous whispers? His daughter Autumn fell victim to the whisperings of a kid named Donny, a name that sounds anything but sinister. Drugs. Addiction. Cliff remembers wanting to punish Donny in horrific fashion. Beat him mercilessly, choke him to death, it didn't matter. Maybe that lingering hatred had drained the last cell of passion from his blood.

He goes to the kitchen. These days it's where he feels most comfortable. He sets the wine glass aside, chops up the mushrooms and rummages in drawers for a wooden spoon. The chicken breast is half thawed. He sets it in the microwave and pushes the timer, slices a small cut of butter into a pan and places the pan on a front burner. He adds olive oil, pours in what remains of the bottle of wine and covers the pan, then leaves the ingredients to simmer and goes to his office and turns on his computer.

As the computer warms up, he stares at the twins' softball trophies on the shelf, five in all. One of them, Autumn, was awarded most valuable player. The trophies represent his most cherished years. Summer says she wants her daughter to see them, but she never brings Christa to the house. Her husband, Kevin, believes the Devil lurks inside the home where prayer isn't a daily ritual, waiting to do mischief. Cliff, indifferent to religion, figures that his son-in-law considers him a heretic.

Cliff notices a fingerprint on the twins' softball picture that sits next to the trophies. Summer holds a bat over her shoulder and Autumn squats beside her, catcher's mitt extended toward the camera. Seeing them together, no one would've suspected they were twins, Summer blonde, Autumn brunette, both smart and each unruly in her own way. He wipes the smudge with his sleeve, replaces the picture and turns to the computer.

He scrolls to a familiar URL for the images of Anna the opera singer and clicks the mouse. Her grainy image opens on the screen. He turns up the volume. She was forty when the performance was filmed. Was her life performing and nothing else? He wonders if she had children. He remembers the school assembly when he first heard that voice deliver the school song– "Where winds blow o'er golden sands and settle in the vale. . ." He spotted her amid the choir and wondered how it was he'd never noticed her before. When the song ended, the student body clapped and sat. He continued standing, hoping she'd notice him. She did.

In the middle of her aria, the phone rings. He lowers the volume.

"Opera again?" Ilene asks. "I can hear it."

"Yes."

"You don't understand a word of it."

He turns off the computer. "Neither do you."

"No. But I don't listen to it. I called to remind you that we're invited to Summer's for dinner. I left a message on the recorder."

"I'm not going."

"Why's that?"

"Because Kevin degrades her and insults us and I can't pretend it's not happening. And because Summer sets up these family things, thinking you and I'll get back together. Besides, it's not the same without Autumn."

"I've told her that you and I have . . . You know, our granddaughter expects you. And what is this about opera?"

"You wouldn't understand." He imagines others looking at the relationship between him and his ex-wife. He knows how strange the arrangement seems to Norma, his office manager, but how many couples reared twins? Just having twin daughters made both their marriage and their divorce unique. Early on, even while breast-feeding, it seemed Ilene became more attached to Summer, while he didn't favor one over the other until Autumn took up softball and he was her coach. He and Ilene got split custody, and each daughter took sides during and after the divorce. Now he and Ilene are congenial ex-spouses who keep their personal lives secret and avoid asking personal questions. He hasn't mentioned his being diagnosed with atrial fibrillation.

"You're probably right." Ilene says. "So, I guess I'll go alone."

"Tell Summer I'm busy. Make something up. Okay?"

"Fine. I'll make up an excuse. Are you still planning to sell the business?"

What's next, he wonders, if he sells his agency? After three decades, it's impossible to feel passionate about peddling insurance, even if you like your clients. "Maybe. Thirty years is a lot of time to do the same thing."

"And what'll you do?"

"Learn Italian, so I can understand the lyrics."

"Don't be funny. You're not good at it."

"Anything you say. Tell Summer I love her."

After their goodbyes, he returns to the kitchen and finds the sauce bubbling. He sprinkles in chopped garlic, stirs the ingredients, adds oregano and stirs again. He thinks of Ilene's pregnancy coming unexpectedly as it did three months after the wedding. It cut short her college career and he became an insurance agent. She returned to college determined to finish. He peddled insurance. Now she's a professor and an understanding, always tolerant ex-spouse. And now he's . . . He doesn't care to dwell on it, but his condition can't be ignored. A fainting spell. A trip to the doctor. "You're in good health," the doctor said, "except for a problem with your heart. I'll refer you to a specialist."

Hearing a pronouncement like that demands self-examination, as does discovering that the girl he once loved found fame on the opera stage. He recalls a lingering kiss beneath a porch light. Anna, the name sings in his head. How easy falling in love with her had been and how impossible. Still, he fantasizes about how different life would have been had he been with her. Or if he'd pursued his real passion.

He forks the breasts into the pan, then places a lid atop.

After eating, he places the dishes and pans in the dishwasher and returns to the computer where he picks out *Anna Gabrisi Sings Rossini*. It was recorded at La Scala. Her image at age thirty dressed in mourning black graces the cover. He wonders if time has touched her as it has him. Hair almost gone, cataract surgery, arthritis in a knee and elbow, and now arrhythmia.

The phone rings. He mutters, then freezes the computer. He expects to hear Summer's voice on the other end, accusing him of ruining the evening. Instead, Autumn says, "Daddy."

He senses panic in her. "What's the matter, honey?"

"Come sign me out and take me to dinner."

"Maybe I have a hot date," he says hoping to make her smile. Her smiles have been few for too long.

"I hope it's not with Mother. Please, I'm serious. I need to get out for an hour or two."

"I'm on my way."

Ψ Ψ Ψ Ψ Ψ Ψ

LAS VEGAS IS NORMALLY a half-hour drive from Boulder City, but traffic is dense along the freeway today. At the Buffalo turnoff, Cliff finds himself trapped behind a driver in a Mercedes Benz SUV who sits talking on a cell phone despite having an open lane. He leans on his horn and a slow moment later the driver of the Mercedes turns slowly onto Buffalo. He pulls around the Mercedes to the middle lane, glares at the driver and is immediately blocked in by cars on either side. His blood pressure rises easily these days, especially in the scorching Mojave heat. The tone of Autumn's voice and her calling him Daddy, instead of Dad, bespoke urgency.

He rings the bell at Montrose Retreat and waits. The woman behind the desk buzzes him in. Autumn waits in the reception room, a magazine in her lap. She sets it aside. At the counter, he signs his name beside where hers is printed in bold letters. The woman says he has to return Autumn in three hours. Lowering her voice, she adds, "No alcohol. No drugs."

He nods, then turns to Autumn and smiles. "You ready?"

She stands. They don't talk until they're in his car. "Where do you want to go?"

She shrugs. "You pick."

"Olive Garden?"

"Jesus, Dad. Anything but that."

He grins. It's a private joke. After one softball game, he treated the entire team to a meal at Olive Garden, and his daughters scolded him. Autumn said, "It's so gauche." He'd tried to explain how, as a boy, he would've been pleased to eat there, that dinner too often had been macaroni and cheese he cooked for his younger brothers and sister.

"Dad, they'll let me out in two weeks for the Fourth of July. The whole weekend. If I have someplace to go or some . . . Can we plan something? Go somewhere?"

"Right now, let's feed you. I'll think about it. You called me Daddy on the phone."

She denies having said it and asks him to take her to Grape Street Station. "I want chicken piccata. Okay?"

"No wine."

"Isn't that why you go there?"

He orders a small salad, and for her sake, doesn't have any wine. She devours the first few bites, then begins picking at her plate. He's curious if it has to do with her addiction, if she's lost her appetite for anything other than drugs? She lays her fork on the plate and stares at him.

"If you don't want to take me somewhere, I understand. I've disappointed Mom and you."

He asks where she'd like to go. She shakes her head. After fielding several ideas, none of which excite her interest, including driving to Los Angeles for a Dodgers' game, he mentions the Hualapai Mountains where he and the girls once stayed in a cabin for a week. He figures it'll make for a good trip, father and daughter again, pals sharing time.

"I remember." Autumn's eyebrows rise. "The summer Mom went to Europe between semesters to . . . What was she studying then?"

He grins. "I'm sure it wasn't opera."

"Let's go." Her voice sounds hopeful. "I mean, I like the idea of baseball, but . . ."

He motions for her to wipe a bit of food from the corner of her mouth. "I'll run it by your mother. See if she wants to go."

She uses the napkin to conceal a smile. "She wouldn't go if we chained her to the bumper of the car."

He knows it's a lie when parents say they love their children equally. It's the same as saying they like all people the same. His favorite was his little beauty, Autumn. He called her that even though, as the girls matured, it was obvious that Summer, blonde with an oval face and magnetic eyes, was the one people were drawn to. It was Autumn's spirit that captured him, the way she tossed off her face-guard to go after a pop-up and her sheer determination to steal a base. She broke her arm once stealing third, but played out the season in a cast crouched behind the plate.

She lifts her fork to take a bite, but stops. She appears on the verge of tearing up. "Dad, what if I can't? I mean, what if I go back to using?"

"Don't think that way."

"I can't think any other way. This is my third time. Why aren't I like Summer?"

"Because you're not. Are you going to take that bite or do I have to eat it?"

"Most people in the home are returnees like me. They go out. They come back."

"They aren't you. Remember how you finished a season with a cast on your arm?"

She nods and bites down on the slice of chicken.

As he watches her eat, he recalls the hours spent watching his girls play softball. Those weekend afternoons and evenings had been his relief from the never-ending insurance hustle. By then he'd built a successful business, driven to do so because he wanted for his family the things his parents failed to do for theirs. He didn't deprive the twins of anything. Even later, as he came to suspect Autumn of using drugs, he gave her money—a mistake he regrets.

"Do you like opera?" he asks.

"You know I listen to country western. No one likes opera."

"Some people do. I do."

"You know what Summer said? She said she didn't want me around Christa. That I'd be a bad influence on my niece. She said it was a good thing I didn't have my own children."

"She didn't mean it. That's just her parroting Kevin. She'll change her mind." What, he wonders, has become of his girls, Summer addicted to religion, Autumn to drugs?

"She was my best friend," Autumn says. "I want to fix it. I want to fix my mistakes."

"You fix them by not repeating them," he says.

"Dad, you sound like a counselor. Did you ever love someone who didn't love you?"

He finds it interesting that she doesn't link her mother to the question. He doesn't have a quick answer or a right one. "How about some creme brûlée?"

AFTER HE LOADS THE cooler with the food, he hesitates, then returns to his office for the sketchbook and box of charcoals he brought when told to take up a hobby. He carries them to the trunk, then looks on the garage shelves for Autumn's backpack. He lifts a box down from the top shelf and when he opens it, he finds pads containing Ilene's notes from her doctoral program. He starts to close the box, but changes his mind and reads a page, every word written in a neat cursive. The notes cover a lecture about a subject called deconstructionism and postmodern social theory. He drops the notepad in the box and sets it aside where he'll remember to get it to Ilene later.

He recalls the day Ilene had been accepted into the PhD program at Bennington to study on a graduate teaching fellowship. She'd said, "You'll have to parent your daughters now." By then the marriage was ready for white flags. Though neither was yet prepared to surrender to the truth, it seemed a mistake to both, all but their daughters. He knows it wasn't easy for Ilene, the years she labored alone at home with the twins while all day and often into the night he was selling policies to get the business started.

Those years of his solo parenting had been his best, and good ones for Ilene as well. He heard it in her voice whenever she called. He suspected her of having an affair with the professor who chaired her dissertation. He wasn't jealous and he never tried to confirm his suspicion.

Now, she's curious about his taking up painting and about his recent interest in opera, but she expresses it by teasing him.

He spots Autumn's backpack and opens it. Inside he finds a health bar that's been in there at least a dozen years. He drops it in the box with Ilene's notes and smiles, knowing that she'll wonder where it came from, but she won't ask. The last items he takes to the car are the CDs. He holds one at arm's length and looks at the picture of Anna on the album cover.

🌵 🌵 🌵 🌵 🌵 🌵

AUTUMN WAITS AT THE door, her overnight bag at her feet. He waves to her through the glass and presses the button. The door lock buzzes. When he steps in, she points to her hiking boots. He recognizes them as a pair he gave her for Christmas when she was twenty and majoring in nursing, the year she met Donny at a New Year's party and dropped out of college and, in a way, life.

"They're old," she says and picks up her overnight bag.

"They're broken in," he says and goes to the counter to sign her out.

He holds the door open and whispers, "Your mother's coming with us."

Autumn jabs an elbow in his side. Her mood's lighter than he's witnessed in weeks, but then the road to Hoover Dam is backed up at the check point. Autumn flips on the radio and scans the stations. She barely speaks during the drive. Her mood seems to have darkened. She races the dial through the stations, stopping no more than a few seconds on each.

"What're you looking for?"

She shrugs. "I don't know. Something not . . . not so . . . I hear those songs and they make me think of getting high."

"I have a couple of CDs in the glove box. Try one."

The line of cars moves forward as she retrieves the cases. She looks at the cover art, a photograph of Anna under the title *La Diva Bella à Paris.*

"It's opera, Dad."

"Yep."

"I mean, really? You want me to listen to opera?"

"Give it a try."

She shrugs and inserts the CD. He taps the accelerator as the line of cars inches forward and Anna's voice, wistful and melodic, begins an aria from *Madama Butterfly.* A moment later, Anna's voice fills the car. Autumn turns up the volume. She sits, head bowed, intent on the music or lost in thought the way she was the evening before he hurried her to the hospital.

He rolls down his window at the security point.

The officer leans toward the open window. "Where are you headed?"

"Kingman. Actually, the mountains."

"Driver's license. And can you turn that down?"

Cliff lowers the volume, then shows his license. The car in front of them moves and the officer nods and signals him through. Autumn raises the volume as the aria reaches its climax. When the last notes die off, she lowers the volume and looks out at the dam.

"I wish I knew the words," she says. "It's so sad."

"I don't know the words, but it's about her killing herself because of a forbidden love."

"God, Dad. Did you have to tell me that? Are the rest of the songs so depressing?"

"It's opera. It's life." Does any opera, he wonders, lament the life of a man who worked all hours and missed meals with the family? Or a marriage that dies because work drives a knife into it?

"What's her name, the singer?"

"Anna Ferrel."

"That's beautiful." She leans back in her seat and closes her eyes.

He pictures her on the verge of falling into a coma as they sped to the emergency room. He kept telling her that they were almost there, assuring her she'd be okay. She'd been living in an apartment with Jess, the latest loser, and waiting tables at Bouchon in the Venetian. Jess lost his job as a craps dealer. Her income went to supporting his OxyContin habit, one that she eventually adopted. She never said if the overdose was accidental or intentional, but at least she called for help before she went comatose. Called him, he reminds himself.

By the time they reach the outskirts of Kingman, Autumn's listening to the final track of a second CD, Anna singing lieder. His daughter seems at peace. He doesn't want to break the spell, but the lanes narrow from three to two and he has to slow the car. Autumn turns off the stereo and tells him she's hungry.

"Sure. We can eat and still get there in time for a hike. Would you like that?"

She shrugs. Counselors cautioned him that her moods would swing and not to push her too hard. "We don't have to hurry," he assures her. "I reserved the cabin."

"No, let's eat fast. I'd like to take a hike," she says.

She goes inside the cabin as he unpacks the car. He's taking the cooler from the trunk when she comes up from behind and asks if she can help. He points to the backpacks resting on the bumper. "Start there."

"You brought two," she says.

"There's two of us."

She lifts one out. "It's mine from when we used to go hiking. You kept it."

"I never got around to cleaning out the garage."

"I can finish unpacking," she says. "Let me be useful."

He's storing food in the refrigerator when she brings in his sketch pad and the box containing charcoal pencils. "What's this?"

"Oh, just a hobby."

"You draw?"

"Thought I'd try."

"Opera and drawing? Maybe you belong in counseling," she says.

"I do. Let's fill the water bottles and go."

"You told me her name was Anna Ferrell. The list of performers says Anna Bella Cabrisi."

He's taken aback because he can't quickly explain that past or its connection to the present. How can he describe his intangible loss or how Anna now seems more real as a voice than she ever was as a tangle of sensuality, a hand he held in the darkened interior of a car? He was merely a boy who could draw with some skill, fated, as were most reared in West Texas, to graduate, hold down a job, and stumble through college a class at a time. Does opera exist for such a boy?

"My mistake."

"You've got four albums with her name on them. Don't you read the credits?"

"Busted," he says and picks up his backpack. Maybe someday he'll tell her about first love's pain, but not now. "I know her from high school."

"She's pretty. Did you–?"

"Let's go. I don't want to lose a day with my little beauty."

They reach a steep incline that leads to a series of switchbacks. The thin air affects his breathing. The cardiologist said if that happened for him to stop and rest. Autumn, unaffected by the climb, keeps a steady pace. He views this as a test of his condition and stays up with her until they leave the tree line where he falls behind. She waits trailside near an overlook. Enormous egg-shaped boulders stretch north about hundred feet. He sheds his pack and leans against the face of a rock.

"Dad, is something the matter?" she asks.

His heart is racing. He takes a long breath, then exhales slowly before saying, "Old and out of shape is all."

"We can go back."

He sees a chance to tell her about the doctor's prognosis and why it's important for him to go on, but she doesn't need any additional burdens on her mind. "We'll go to the top."

"I wanted you to know I'm going back to college," she says. "After rehab."

In her expression, he sees signs of the old determination that drove her to steal bases and chase pop-ups. "Good. We can manage that. What's tuition run these days?"

"No. I don't want help, not that kind. I need to do it on my own."

"Okay. But if you do."

"The rocks are amazing." Autumn turns and walks toward the overlook.

"Wait," he says.

She looks back over her shoulder and smiles.

He was thirty-two when he started his business, twelve- to sixteen-hour days for ten years. After the fledgling years of struggle, the business ran itself and the girls were his alone for nearly eight years. He had that.

"You know I enjoyed being a parent?"

"Really? That's the nicest thing you've ever said to me."

A breeze drifts up from the canyon and Autumn weaves her way across the boulders. He drinks from his water bottle and watches her scurry to the top of the farthest boulder, where she stands outlined by the desert sky. He wants to tell her not so close. One wrong step could . . . A vagrant thought crosses his mind. His death's worth a half million, but what's his life worth? Even as the doctor put him on a regimen of pills for blood pressure and daily aspirin and warned him to take the arrhythmia seriously, death seemed abstract, just as it seemed abstract when he'd hand a pen to a client to sign a policy contract. Now it's not abstract.

She turns and shouts, "Come see."

He goes slowly to her. The two of them stare out for a time, then return to their backpacks and climb the trail to its summit.

🌵 🌵 🌵 🌵 🌵 🌵

CLIFF SETTLES HIMSELF ATOP the concrete table and looks up where the sun angles down from the west. The nearest peak rises another thousand feet. He decides that although mountains have been drawn since the days men rendered images on cave walls, he'll give it a try. After all, it's just geometry and geology, a few trees tossed in. Autumn steps out of the cabin and comes up beside him. He holds the sketch pad away, so she can't see.

"Dad, you're silly. Did you know your face went white up there?"

He shakes his head. She asks for the car keys.

"You plan on driving somewhere?"

"Do you trust me?"

He hands her the keys and she goes to the car. Instead of starting the engine, she inserts a CD in the stereo and the opening orchestration to *Otello* sounds over the speakers. She turns up the volume and walks to a boulder near the tree line. Desdemona sings of her joy at Otello's return. She sings it the same as when he listened to the aria before, but Cliff hears it differently this time, the glorious high notes, not the girl he knew singing, but the art behind it.

Autumn unties the bow holding her hair and shakes her ponytail free. She sits facing north, her arms wrapped over her knees. He flips to a blank sheet. As he does, a bull elk emerges out of the trees, followed by three cows. Then a fourth cow steps from the shadows and calmly begins grazing on the bushes at the camp's edge. Autumn looks back, her face alight in a way Cliff hasn't seen in years. Her eyes telegraph his thoughts. Don't move. Don't breathe. He begins putting charcoal to paper.

"She's beautiful." Autumn turns her attention again to the elk now grazing some ten feet from her.

In the background, Desdemona vows her love for Otello. The bull watches two ungainly calves emerge from the tree line and join the cows in grazing. Occasionally, the animals look up and regard Autumn and Cliff with regal indifference.

Autumn glances back again. "Look at her, at them," he says.

The charcoal travels over the paper forming lines and curls. Images of his daughter, the elk and the rugged forest take shape on the coarse surface, not as they might in a photograph, but as the eye and hand intend when he puts them on canvas as a singular gathering of life.

"Dad, are you drawing me?"

"Keep looking at them," he says. "Look at the divas."

Then suddenly, Autumn stands and walks in the animals' direction. He thinks to call her back. Elk, he's heard, can be dangerous. But they merely gaze at her as she nears. They make no effort to flee. Nor do they seem in a mood to attack. Then she's among them, sitting herself at their center. She plucks at the loose bunch grass with her pale fingers as the huge animals graze the ground around her. She looks back at him. Her lips part into a wide and carefree smile.

He can tell her nothing about the heartache of young love. He flips to a new page and begins sketching. The images form seemingly on their own. He's no longer a man hearing an urgent whisper inside his head to get the client to sign for a policy, or the man whose lost confidence in what a charcoal stick can do on paper or a brush on canvas. He's not a man whose heart has aged too fast. He's a witness to miracles.

acknowledgments

The author would first like to express his gratitude to the publisher and editors at Baobab Press for their patience and multiple contributions in bringing this collection to publication, in particular he cites Ms. Margaret Dalrymple, who has, over many years in several ways, promoted his writing efforts.

He also expresses his thanks to the editors and publishers of journals and anthologies who have recognized or published the following stories contained in this collection: "Life Is a Country Western Song," a finalist in the 2016 *Narrative* open story competition; "Sheets," published in the anthology *Just to Watch Him Die*, Virginia Avenue Press, 2012; "The Boy Who Smelled Colors," "In the End," and "A Cop Story," *Red Rock Review*, Spring 2015, Fall 2016, and Fall 2017 respectively; "The Road to Mandalay Without Laughter," *The McGuffin*, Special Edition 2000; "The Disassembled Part" and "Divas," *Nevada Review*, Fall 2012 and Fall 2013 respectively; "A Fine Open Space," *Iron Horse Review*, Trifecta, 2014. And a final thanks to Mary Sojourner, whose comments have been helpful over the past two decades.

about the author

H. Lee Barnes, memoirist, novelist, and short story writer, is the author of ten books. His short works have received the Willamette Fiction Award and the Arizona Authors Association fiction prize. In 2009, he was inducted into the Nevada Writers Hall of Fame, and in 2013 he received an excellence in the arts award from the Vietnam Veterans of America for his body of work. His varied careers include working as a deputy sheriff, a private investigator, a narcotics agent, a casino dealer, and a college professor. He now lives in the Hualapai Valley in Northern Arizona.

The body of *Life Is a Country Western Song* is set in Garamond, an old-style serif typeface created by sixteenth-century Parisian engraver Claude Garamont. The cover headers are set in Plantagenet Cherokee, a transitional serif typeface created by Ross Mills in 1996, and the story headers have been set in Futura PT, a geometric sans-serif typeface designed by Paul Renner released in 1927 and based on geometric shapes, especially the circle.

Typeset and design by Baobab Press.

CPSIA information can be obtained
at www.ICGtesting.com
Printed in the USA
LVHW012249150119
604063LV00002B/3/P